# ALEX KNIGHT

## AND THE

# DARK STORM

ANDROR M. THOMPSON

**ALEX KNIGHT**

AND THE

**DARK STORM**

COPYRIGHT © 2024 Andror M. Thompson

All rights reserved. No part of this book may be used or reproduced in any manner whatsoever without written permission except in the case of brief quotations embodied in critical articles and reviews.

# Contents

**Prologue** ... 1

**Chapter One** ... 4
The Rise Of Alex & The Realm Defenders

**Chapter Two** ... 20
Shadows Of The City: Unveiling The Hood's Reign

**Chapter Three** ... 36
Invitation To The Portal

**Chapter Four** ... 51
Betrayal Unveiled

**Chapter Five** ... 65
Adventure At The Theme Park: Journey Of Thrills And Wonder

**Chapter Six** ... 84
Zyro's Attack

**Chapter Seven** ... 96
The Search For The Component

**Chapter Eight** ... 119
The Puzzle In The Palace

**Chapter Nine** ... 141
Dark Storm In London

**Chapter Ten** ... 155
"Embers Of Hope: A Saga Of Fire, Fury, And Triumph"

# PROLOGUE

A millennia ago, the Battle of Dimensions raged across the cosmic expanse, a clash of titans that would echo through the ages. Vesta, the fearless guardian of Esmeria, stood firm against the evil warlord Zyro, once a loyal warrior of Esmeria, now consumed by envy and ambition. Zyro's visage twisted by dark magic appeared as a monstrous hybrid of human and beast, clad in obsidian armour that gleamed with an otherworldly sheen.

"You dare to stand against me, Vesta?" Zyro's voice dripped with contempt, his words laced with the sinister undertones of his twisted ambitions. "You, who were once my ally, now foolishly believe you can thwart my plans?"

Vesta squared her shoulders, undaunted by Zyro's menacing presence. "I stand not for myself, but for the people of Esmeria, whom you seek to subjugate with your darkness," she retorted, her voice resolute like the steadfast mountains that loomed in the distance.

Zyro laughed, "The people of Esmeria are but pawns in the grand tapestry of fate," he declared, his eyes blazing with an unholy fervour. "Their feeble attempts to resist me only hasten their inevitable doom."

With a sweep of his clawed hand, Zyro summoned forth a legion of dark storm creatures, their twisted forms writhing with malevolent energy. "Behold the might of my army, Vesta," he proclaimed, his voice booming like the roar of a tempest. "No force in the cosmos can withstand the power that I wield!"

With his long black hair cascading like a shadowy waterfall and his eyes burning with an unholy glow, Zyro commanded legions of dark storm creatures, shape-shifting entities born from the depths of madness.

These shadowy abominations, fueled by the despair and anguish of Esmerian citizens, roamed the land like harbingers of chaos, leaving a wake of destruction and decay in their path. Their mere presence cast a pall of fear and unease upon the land, driving the inhabitants of Esmeria to the brink of madness. Yet, their insidious influence extended only to the Esmerians; humans from Earth remained unaffected, though they could not escape the suffocating tendrils of fear that coiled around them in the presence of these creatures.

The battle reached a crescendo of cosmic proportions in the final confrontation between Vesta and Zyro. With every clash of their weapons, the very fabric of reality trembled, as if the universe itself held its breath. In a moment of desperation, Zyro unleashed the full extent of his dark power, morphing into a colossal monstrosity that loomed over the battlefield like a harbinger of apocalypse.

But Vesta, the indomitable guardian of Esmeria, stood resolute against the onslaught, her determination unwavering even in the face of such overwhelming odds. With a thunderous roar, she banished Zyro to the nether realms, casting him adrift between time and space for eternity or so she believed.

In the present day, Esmeria thrived under Vesta's benevolent rule, a vibrant realm where magic and wonder intertwined. The Battle of Dimensions had become a distant memory, commemorated each year with a grand celebration—a magical otherworldly theme park where joy and laughter filled the air.

Lyra, a young and spirited denizen of Esmeria, couldn't shake the feeling of unease that gripped her heart as a troublesome storm swept across the horizon. Dark clouds roiled ominously, and a chill wind whispered tales of ancient evils stirring once more.

"Could it be...Zyro?" Lyra whispered; her voice tinged with apprehension.

Vesta, while in her palace, her eyes shimmering with ancient wisdom, placed a reassuring hand on Lyra's shoulder. "Fear not, child," she said, her voice a soothing melody amid the tempest. "Zyro is lost to the annals of time, his dark legacy nothing more than a fading nightmare. This storm is but a natural phenomenon, a passing tempest that heralds no ill omen."

Despite Vesta's assurance, Lyra felt that Vesta wasn't telling her the entire truth as a means not to worry Esmerian people. Why did Lyra have the nagging feelings in the depths of her stomach that she should be worried?

# CHAPTER ONE

## THE RISE OF ALEX & THE REALM DEFENDERS

It was a new season, and Alex Knight, the group's charismatic leader, walked with a confident swagger alongside his friends, now famously known as "Alex & The Realm Defenders." His wit and humour were on full display as he cracked jokes and bantered with his companions on their way to the prestigious TV studio for their interview. Despite his humorous facade, Alex could easily switch to a serious demeanour when the situation demanded it, a quality that had proven invaluable during their battles against nefarious villains.

Marcus, the lovable goofball of the group, seemed to be in his element as he unleashed a barrage of hilarious one-liners and slapstick antics, much to the amusement of his friends. His infectious laughter filled the air, earning him cheers and applause from fans outside the studio. Clad in a comfortable grey hoodie, Marcus moved with boundless energy, his playful dedemeanourddding a sense of levity to the group's dynamic.

Scarlette, the brainy and sensible member of the group, observed her friends' antics with a knowing smile. Despite her intelligence and practicality, Scarlette had a playful side to her personality, often indulging in witty banter with Alex and joining in Marcus's antics with a chuckle. Her braided hair swayed gently as she walked, complementing her casual yet stylish ensemble consisting of a vibrant red jacket. However, her trusting nature sometimes made her susceptible to the group's pranks and practical jokes, much to her chagrin.

Nevertheless, Scarlette's level-headedness and quick thinking had often saved the day, earning her the respect and admiration of her friends.

As they made their way to enter the prestigious TV studio for their interview. The fame that had followed their victory over Ruok, the nefarious villain who had threatened the very existence of their world, seemed surreal to them. They had become heroes overnight, their names plastered across headlines, their faces adorning posters and merchandise in every corner of the city.

The group sauntered down the street, Alex leading the way with his trademark confidence. "Alright, team, ready to knock 'em dead?"

Scarlette shot him a wry smile. "Let's just hope your charm doesn't distract the interviewer too much, Alex."

Marcus, always the jester, chimed in with a chuckle. "Yeah, we might end up spending the whole time discussing your favourite pizza toppings!"

Alex grinned back. "Hey, pizza is a universal language, Marcus. You should know that."

Scarlette couldn't resist teasing. "As long as it doesn't overshadow the real heroes of the story."

Marcus playfully nudged Scarlette. "Oh, come on, Scarlette,

we all know I'm the real hero here!"

Scarlette rolled her eyes, but there was affection in her gaze. "Of course, Marcus. Who else would keep us laughing in the face of danger?"

Alex chuckled, the sound warm and reassuring. "That's right. We're a team, and each brings something invaluable to the table."

Marcus puffed out his chest dramatically. "Well, of course! With my wit, Scarlette's brains, and Alex's... well, charm, we're unstoppable!"

Alex threw an arm around Marcus's shoulder, laughing. "Careful, Marcus, your ego might not fit through the studio door!"

Scarlette shook her head, a fond smile tugging at her lips. "Let's just focus on getting through the interview without any major mishaps, shall we?"

As they entered the studio, the atmosphere was electric. Cameras flashed, reporters buzzed with excitement, and fans clamoured for a glimpse of their heroes. Alex felt a surge of pride mixed with unease as he realized the weight of their newfound celebrity status.

The interview went smoothly at first. The host, a charismatic figure with a winning smile, guided them through questions about their epic battle with Ruok, their strategies for victory, and their plans for the future. Alex and his friends answered with humility and confidence, grateful for the opportunity to share their story with the world.

The host leaned forward with a smile. "So, Alex, what was your strategy during the showdown with Ruok?"

Alex leaned in, his eyes sparkling with determination. "Our strategy? It was all about calculated risks and seizing the right opportunities. We knew we had to hit Ruok hard and fast, but also stay adaptable to his moves."

Scarlette nodded beside him, adding, "Exactly. We couldn't afford to let our emotions get the best of us. Every decision had to be precise."

Marcus, ever the optimist, interjected, "But hey, let's not forget the power of teamwork! We might have had our differences, but when it came down to it, we had each other's backs."

The host turned to Marcus with a grin. "And how did you maintain morale during the toughest moments?"

Marcus beamed; his enthusiasm infectious. "Oh, that's easy! Laughter is the best medicine, right? So, I made sure to keep the jokes coming, even when things got hairy."

Scarlette couldn't help but smirk. "Yes, because nothing boosts morale like Marcus's questionable sense of humour."

Alex chuckled, coming to Marcus's defence. "Hey, it worked, didn't it? Besides, Scarlette here was always the voice of reason, keeping us grounded when things got too chaotic."

Scarlette nodded a hint of pride in her expression. "Someone had to make sure we didn't fly off the rails completely."

But as the interview progressed, cracks began to appear in the façade that had held their group together during their adventures. Ego, that insidious foe that lurked within the hearts of even the noblest heroes, reared its ugly head.

It started with a harmless comment from one of Alex's friends about the number of enemies they had defeated during their quest. Another friend, eager to assert their contribution to the team's success, chimed in with a boast about their superior combat skills. Before long, the interview devolved into a heated debate, each member of the group vying for the spotlight and seeking validation for their achievements.

the tension in the room seemed to thicken with each passing moment. Scarlette shifted uncomfortably in her seat, exchanging uneasy glances with Marcus and Alex as they navigated the minefield of their egos.

Marcus, always eager to assert his prowess, cleared his throat, his voice laced with a hint of arrogance.

"You know, it's not just about the number of enemies we've defeated. It's about the strategy, the precision. That's what sets us apart."

Scarlette raised an eyebrow, her tone dripping with sarcasm.

"Oh, please. Last time I checked, victory wasn't determined by who could boast the loudest."

Alex, sensing the tension escalating, attempted to diffuse the situation with a forced chuckle.

"Come on, guys, let's not turn this into a competition. We're a team, remember?"

But Marcus wasn't about to back down, his competitive spirit ignited.

"A team, sure. But let's not forget who's been leading the charge in battle, who's been keeping us one step ahead of our enemies."

Scarlette bristled at Marcus's implication, her voice growing sharper. "And who's been there to clean up the mess when your reckless tactics put us all in danger?"

Marcus scoffed, his pride wounded. "Oh, please, Scarlette. You act like you're the only one who's ever had to make tough calls in the heat of battle."

The room crackled with tension as the argument intensified, each word a weapon in the battle of egos. Alex watched helplessly as his friends, once bound by a shared purpose, allowed their pride to drive a wedge between them.

"Guys, enough!" Alex finally interjected, his voice cutting through the escalating argument. "We're supposed to be a team, remember? We're stronger together than we are apart."

But Marcus and Scarlette seemed deaf to his pleas, their egos too entrenched to back down. As the argument reached its boiling point, Alex couldn't help but feel a pang of sadness. Their friendship, once unbreakable, now hung in the balance, threatened by the very egos they had sworn to overcome.

Alex watched in dismay as his friends, once united in their mission to protect their world, allowed their egos to drive a wedge between them. He tried to intervene, to remind them of the importance of teamwork and solidarity, but his words were lost in the noise of self-aggrandizement and one-upmanship.

By the time the interview drew to a close, the tension among the group was palpable. They posed for a final photo, forced smiles masking their inner turmoil, before making a hasty exit from the studio.

Outside, the fans still clamoured for autographs and selfies, oblivious to the rift that had formed within their beloved heroes. Alex couldn't help but feel a pang of sadness as he realized that their fame had come at a cost, threatening to tear apart the very fabric of their friendship.

But as they walked away from the studio, their footsteps echoing in the empty streets, Alex knew that they would find a way to overcome this obstacle, just as they had overcome countless challenges before. For they were not just a team of heroes bound by duty, but friends bound by something far stronger: their unbreakable bond forged in the fires of adversity.

It was a crisp sunny afternoon, and Alex Knight found himself surrounded by the familiar sights and sounds of his beloved hometown. The aroma of sizzling burgers wafted through the air, drawing him and his friends to their usual hangout spot – a quaint little diner nestled in the heart of the city.

As they settled into their usual booth, laughter, and chatter filled the air, mingling with the excited buzz of fans who had gathered outside, eager for a chance to catch a glimpse of their favourite heroes. Alex and his friends, now widely recognized as "Alex & The Realm Defenders," had become local celebrities after their triumphant victory over Ruok, the villainous force that had threatened their world.

Despite the warm reception from their adoring fans, tension lingered among the group. The aftermath of their recent interview at the TV studio still hung heavy in the air, casting an impression over their usually jovial gatherings. The egos that had clashed during the interview seemed to have followed them to their sanctuary, threatening to disrupt the camaraderie that had once bound them together.

As they nibbled on their super burgers, the conversation turned to their plans for the future, particularly their burgeoning YouTube business. Ideas flew back and forth, and each member of the group was eager to share their vision for the channel and stake their claim to its success. However, a sense of unease simmered beneath the surface as they struggled to find common ground amidst their differing opinions.

As they savoured the juicy burgers, the conversation shifted to their aspirations for their burgeoning YouTube venture. Alex leaned forward, his eyes gleaming with excitement as he shared his vision for the channel.

"Imagine it, guys," he began, his voice brimming with enthusiasm. "We could document our adventures, share behind-the-scenes footage, interact with our fans – the possibilities are endless!"

Marcus nodded, a grin spreading across his face. "Yeah, and we could do tutorials on combat techniques, share tips and tricks for levelling up – you know, stuff that our fans would appreciate."

Scarlette's eyes lit up with inspiration. "And don't forget about the vlogs! We could give our viewers a glimpse into our daily lives, show them the faces behind the masks."

But as they delved deeper into their plans, a sense of tension began to creep into the conversation. Each member of the group had their ideas about the direction the channel should take, and conflicting opinions threatened to derail their discussion.

"I don't know, guys," Marcus said, furrowing his brow in thought. "I think we should focus more on the action-packed content – you know, the stuff that gets people's adrenaline pumping."

Scarlette shook her head, her expression determined.

"But we can't neglect the storytelling aspect. Our fans want to feel like they're a part of our journey, not just spectators watching from the sidelines."

Alex, caught in the middle, tried to mediate. "Why can't we have both? Action-packed content with a strong narrative thread – that's what sets us apart from other channels."

But finding common ground proved to be more challenging than they had anticipated. As the discussion dragged on, frustrations mounted, and tempers flared.

"We need to figure this out, guys," Alex insisted, his voice tinged with urgency. "Our YouTube channel could be a game-changer for us – but only if we're all on the same page."

Scarlette sighed, running a hand through her hair in frustration.

"I know, Alex. I just want what's best for the channel, you know?"

Marcus nodded, his expression thoughtful. "Yeah, me too. Maybe we should take some time to think about it, and come back with fresh ideas."

With a collective nod of agreement, they tabled the discussion for the time being, each member of the group retreating into their thoughts. As they finished their burgers in silence, Alex couldn't help but wonder if they would ever find the common ground they so desperately sought.

Suddenly, their discussion was interrupted by the arrival of Lucas, a rival of Alex, accompanied by Breezy and Brian. Lucas sauntered over with a smirk, his eyes glinting with mischief as he addressed Alex.

"Well, well, well, if it isn't the mighty Alex and his band of misfits," Lucas sneered, his voice dripping with disdain. "Still riding high on your fifteen minutes of fame, I see."

Alex clenched his jaw, his fists tightening involuntarily at the sight of Lucas and his cohorts. Breezy, once Alex's girlfriend, looked downcast, her gaze flickering between Alex and Lucas. Brian, always eager to please Lucas, stood by silently, a smug grin playing on his lips.

Ignoring Lucas's taunts, Alex attempted to steer the conversation back to safer ground, but Lucas was relentless in his pursuit of provocation.

"So, Alex I heard about your little breakup with Breezy," Lucas continued a malicious glint in his eye. "Seems like she finally came to her senses and realized she deserves better than you."

The words hit Alex like a sucker punch, his heart constricting with a mixture of anger and hurt. He felt the familiar surge of adrenaline coursing through his veins, urging him to lash out in response to Lucas's cruel jabs. But this time, he resisted the urge, knowing that giving in to his anger would only play into Lucas's hands.

With a steely resolve, Alex pushed himself away from the table, his hands trembling with suppressed rage. He met Lucas's gaze with a defiant glare, his voice low and controlled despite the turmoil raging within him.

"I'm not going to let you bait me into a fight, Lucas," Alex growled, his words laced with barely contained fury. "You're not worth my time or my energy."

Lucas scoffed, his smirk widening into a mocking grin as he watched Alex's retreating figure. Breezy, her cheeks flushed with shame, reached out to Alex, her voice trembling with remorse.

"Alex, I'm sorry," she whispered, her eyes brimming with unshed tears. "I never meant to hurt you."

But Alex was already gone, his footsteps echoing in the space where he had stood moments before. The tension hung thick in the air, casting a pall over the once lively atmosphere as Alex's friends exchanged uneasy glances, unsure of how to mend the rift that had formed between them.

Outside the diner, the city buzzed with life, oblivious to the turmoil brewing within its streets. Alex walked alone, his thoughts consumed by the betrayal he had endured and the uncertain path that lay ahead. But amidst the darkness that threatened to engulf him, a glimmer of hope flickered in the depths of his soul – a determination to rise above the petty squabbles and forge a new path forward, one defined not by ego or rivalry, but by the unbreakable bonds of friendship and solidarity.

Alex arrived home; the weight of the day's events still heavy on his shoulders. As he stepped through the front door, the familiar scent of home enveloped him, momentarily easing the tension in his muscles. He greeted his parents with a forced smile, their concerned gazes not escaping his notice.

"Alex, sweetheart, how was your interview?" his mother, Joanna Knight inquired, her voice tinged with a mixture of pride and worry.

"It was fine, Mum," Alex replied with a shrug, not wanting to burden her with the details of the tension that had soured their moment of triumph.

His stepfather, Paul, observed him quietly from his favourite armchair, a knowing glint in his eyes. Paul had always been stern in Alex's life, his imposing presence tempered by moments of quiet understanding. Despite their occasional clashes, Alex knew that Paul cared for him deeply, a fact that he often took for granted.

"Alex, there's something we need to talk about," Paul said, his voice grave as he motioned for Alex to take a seat beside him.

Alex's heart sank as he recognized the seriousness in Paul's tone. He braced himself for a lecture about responsibility and humility, expecting Paul to reprimand him for his behaviour during the interview.

"Your mother, Joanna Knight and I have noticed that you've been neglecting your chores lately," Paul began, his words measured but firm. "You know that being part of a team means fulfilling your responsibilities, both on and off the battlefield."

Alex felt a surge of frustration rising within him, his temper flaring at the perceived injustice of Paul's words. He opened his mouth to protest, to defend himself against what he saw as an unfair accusation, but Paul held up a hand to silence him.

"Listen, Alex," Paul continued, his voice softening as he placed a comforting hand on Alex's shoulder. "I know that fame and success can be overwhelming, but it's important not to lose sight of what truly matters in life. Your mother and I are proud of everything you've accomplished, but we also want you to remember where you come from and the values that we've instilled in you."

Alex's anger ebbed away, replaced by a sense of guilt and remorse. He realized that Paul was right, that he had allowed his newfound fame to cloud his judgment and neglect his duties at home.

"I'm sorry, Paul," Alex murmured, his voice barely above a whisper. "You're right. I've been so caught up in being a hero that I forgot to be a responsible son."

Paul smiled, his eyes twinkling with warmth and

understanding. "It's okay, Alex. We all make mistakes. The important thing is that we learn from them and strive to do better next time."

As Alex and Paul shared a heartfelt moment of reconciliation, Alex's mum watched from the sidelines, her eyes shining with pride and love. Despite the challenges they faced as a family, she knew that they would always find a way to come together and support each other through thick and thin.

Alex's stepdad, Paul, sat on the edge of the couch, his face drawn with concern as he gazed at the family photos adorning the wall. His thoughts were consumed by the daunting news he had received earlier that day, the weight of it heavy on his shoulders. He had been diagnosed with cancer, a diagnosis he hadn't yet found the courage to share with Alex.

Joanna, Alex's mum, joined Paul on the couch, her hand reaching out to rest gently on his knee. She could see the turmoil etched on his face, and she knew that they needed to talk, even if the conversation would be one of the hardest they'd ever had.

"Paul, we can't keep this from Alex any longer," Joanna said softly, her voice tinged with sadness. "He deserves to know what's going on, especially since it's going to affect all of us."

Paul sighed, his heart heavy with the weight of the truth he had been hiding. "I know, Joanna. I just don't know how to tell him. I don't want to worry him any more than he already is."

Joanna nodded in understanding, her fingers intertwining with Paul's as she sought to offer him comfort. "We'll find the right words together, Paul. Alex is stronger than you think, and he deserves to be a part of this journey with us."

Later that evening, as Alex sat alone in his room, the events of the day weighed heavily on his mind. He couldn't shake the feeling of disappointment in himself for letting his ego get the best of him, for losing sight of the values that had guided him throughout his journey as a hero.

Suddenly, his thoughts were interrupted by a soft knock on the door. Alex looked up to see his mother standing in the doorway, her expression gentle and reassuring.

"Can I come in, sweetheart?" she asked, her voice soft with concern.

Alex nodded, a lump forming in his throat as he struggled to find the right words to express his emotions. His mother crossed the room and sat beside him on the bed, wrapping him in a warm embrace.

"I know today was tough for you, Alex," she murmured, her voice soothing in the quiet of the room. "But I want you to know that your father and I are here for you, no matter what."

Tears pricked at the corners of Alex's eyes as he leaned into his mother's embrace, the weight of his emotions finally breaking through the facade of strength he had maintained throughout the day.

"I'm sorry, Mum," he whispered, his voice choked with emotion. "I messed up today. I let my ego get the best of me, and I hurt the people I care about."

His mother held him tighter, her love and support a comforting balm to his wounded soul. "It's okay, sweetheart. We all make mistakes. What's important is that you recognize them and strive to do better next time."

# CHAPTER TWO

## SHADOWS OF THE CITY: UNVEILING THE HOOD'S REIGN

As Alex's mother left his room, her words of comfort still lingering in the air, he found himself alone once more, the weight of his emotions pressing down on him like a suffocating blanket. Despite his parents' reassurances, the turmoil within him refused to abate, the pain of his recent experiences gnawing at his soul with relentless persistence.

With a heavy sigh, Alex slumped back against the pillows, his thoughts a tangled mess of confusion and despair. The events of the day replayed in his mind like a broken record, each painful memory serving as a stark reminder of his vulnerabilities and shortcomings.

He couldn't shake the feeling of emptiness that threatened to consume him, the hollow ache of loneliness echoing through the empty expanse of his room. It was in moments like these, when the facade of strength he projected to the world crumbled away, that Alex felt truly lost, adrift in a sea of uncertainty and self-doubt.

As he lay in the darkness, his mind awash with tumultuous thoughts, Alex's thoughts turned to Breezy, the girl who had once held his heart in her hand. Their relationship had been a whirlwind of passion and intensity, a rollercoaster ride of highs and lows that had ultimately ended in heartbreak and betrayal.

The memory of their breakup still lingered fresh in Alex's mind, a wound that refused to heal despite the passage of time. He couldn't help but wonder what might have been if things had turned out differently if he had been able to forgive and forget the pain of Breezy's betrayal.

But deep down, Alex knew that some wounds ran too deep to ever truly mend, that the scars left behind by betrayal were a constant reminder of the fragility of trust and the consequences of misplaced loyalty. He remembered his last adventures in Esmeria and he's already missingthemt, as he was reminiscing, he flashed back to Vesta, Dippy and Lyra. The thought of him going to the other world lingers in his mind but he realized he need to face problem without running away and moreso, Vesta has not invited him and his friends, as he promised to go with them, but he could do it with the magically delicious Esmerian strawberry brew.

the Strawberry Brew Float, a familiar favourite, tasted entirely new in the enchanting realm. The strawberry flavours burst forth like a cascade of sweet and tart notes, each sip an adventure in itself.

As they indulged in their sumptuous feast, the restaurant seemed to come alive with a special energy, as if the food itself was imbued with the essence of Esmeira. Each bite transported them further into a world of delight and wonder, a place where their senses were heightened and their taste buds rejoiced.

Amid their laughter and joyful chatter, they couldn't help but appreciate the way the flavours resonated with the vibrant ambience of the restaurant. It was as if every dish told a story, and with each bite, they were uncovering a new chapter of Esmeira's culinary magic.

As if on cue with is long thought, Alex's phone lit up with a familiar notification, he picked up the device, his heart sinking as he saw Breezy's name flashing on the screen once more.

For a moment, Alex hesitated, his thumb hovering over the answer button as he wrestled with conflicting emotions. A part of him longed to hear her voice, to seek closure in the aftermath of their breakup, while another part recoiled at the thought of reopening old wounds and revisiting past hurts.

In the end, curiosity won out, and the desperate need to find closure outweighed his better judgment. With a trembling hand, Alex answered the call, his voice wary as he spoke.

"Breezy?"

"Alex, it's me," came Breezy's voice on the other end of the line, her tone hesitant but tinged with desperation.

Alex felt a surge of conflicting emotions rise within him, his heart torn between longing and resentment. "What do you want, Breezy?" he asked, his voice tinged with bitterness.

"I... I miss you, Alex," Breezy admitted, her voice trembling with emotion. "I miss us."

Alex's heart clenched at the sound of her voice, a flood of memories washing over him like a tidal wave. "You miss us?"

he repeated incredulously. "After what you did?"

Breezy's response was immediate, her voice defensive and tinged with indignation. "It wasn't like that, Alex. You have to understand, I was going through a rough time, and I made a mistake. But that doesn't mean we can't work things out."

Alex felt a surge of frustration welling up within him, his patience wearing thin at Breezy's refusal to take accountability for her actions. "A mistake?" he retorted, his voice tinged with bitterness. "Breezy, cheating on someone isn't a mistake. It's a choice, a betrayal of trust. And I can't just pretend like it never happened."

There was a moment of tense silence between them, the weight of their unresolved issues hanging heavy in the air. Alex knew that this conversation was going nowhere, that Breezy was incapable of understanding the pain she had caused him.

"Goodbye, Breezy," Alex said finally, his voice devoid of emotion as he ended the call, cutting off any further attempts at reconciliation.

As he set his phone aside, Alex felt a wave of desolation washes over him, the reality of his situation hit him like a ton of bricks. The pressure of fame, the heartache of his breakup with Breezy, and the rift with his friends weighed heavily on his shoulders, threatening to engulf him in a sea of despair.

It was then that a soft knock on the door roused Alex from his reverie, and he looked up to see his parents standing in the doorway, their expressions filled with concern and empathy.

"Alex, sweetheart, can we talk?" his mother asked softly, her voice a soothing balm to his troubled soul.

Alex nodded silently, inviting them into his room as they settled in beside him, their presence a comforting anchor amidst the storm.

"We know things have been tough for you lately, Alex," his father began, his voice gentle but firm. "But we want you to know that we're here for you, no matter what."

His mother reached out, her hand finding his and squeezing it reassuringly. "Fame isn't everything, Alex. It's easy to get caught up in the allure of recognition and success, but it's important to appreciate the things in regular life that most take for granted."

Alex felt a lump form in his throat as he listened to his parents' words of wisdom, their unconditional love a source of strength and reassurance in his darkest moments. He realized that amidst the chaos of his life, he had neglected to appreciate the simple joys and blessings that surrounded him.

"You're right, Mum, Dad," Alex admitted, his voice choked with emotion. "I've been so focused on chasing fame and success that I forgot to appreciate the people who genuinely care about me."

His parents smiled warmly, their love and support a beacon of hope in the darkness. "We just want you to be happy, Alex," his mother said softly. "And sometimes, happiness can be found in the simplest of things – in the love of family, in the laughter of friends, and the beauty of everyday life."

As he sat in his room reflecting on the events of the day, Alex's phone buzzed with a notification. He glanced at the screen to see a message from Marcus, one of his closest friends and fellow Realm Defenders.

"Hey man, can we talk?" the message read, the words tinged with a sense of urgency.

Curious, Alex quickly replied, agreeing to meet Marcus at their favourite hangout spot later that evening. As he made his way to the meeting, Alex couldn't help but wonder what his friend wanted to discuss. He quickly got up from his bed to see his friend to settle their differences.

When he arrived at the diner, the usual spot. Marcus was already waiting for him, a solemn expression on his usually jovial face. Without a preamble, Marcus launched into the reason for their meeting.

"Alex, I've been doing some thinking," Marcus began, his voice tinged with concern. "About what happened during the interview, about the way we let our egos get in the way of our friendship."

Alex nodded in understanding; his memories of the tense confrontation still fresh in his mind. "Yeah, I've been thinking about that too," he admitted, his voice tinged with regret.

Marcus sighed, running a hand through his hair in frustration. "Look, Alex, I know we've had our differences, but at the end of the day, we're still a team. We're still friends. And I don't want to let something stupid like ego come between us."

Alex felt a surge of gratitude towards his friend, touched by Marcus's sincerity and willingness to mend their fractured friendship. "I agree, Marcus," he said earnestly, a weight lifting off his shoulders. "I don't want to lose what we have because of a stupid argument."

"Yeah, Scarlette added, her voice soft with sincerity. "It's been too long since we've been together."

Alex felt a surge of gratitude towards his friends, touched by their willingness to give him another chance. yes guys too," he admitted, his voice tinged with regret. "I know things got heated between us, but I don't want to let that come between our friendship."

Marcus nodded in agreement, a hint of a smile playing on his lips. "Yeah, me neither," he replied. "Life's too short to hold grudges, right?"

Scarlette chimed in, her eyes sparkling with warmth. "Exactly. We're stronger together than we are apart."

As they sat together in the diner, laughter and conversation flowing freely between them "Wow, Marcus, I haven't been to an arcade in ages. Thanks for suggesting this place," Alex exclaimed as they stepped into the vibrant arcade, the flashing lights and lively atmosphere immediately captivating him.

"No problem, Alex," Marcus smirked, glancing around at the array of games and attractions. "Figured we could use a change of scenery for our talk. Plus, it's a great place to relax and unwind."

Alex nodded in agreement, already feeling the tension easing from his shoulders as they walked further into the arcade. "Beats meeting at our usual spot. Plus, who can resist a good round of skeeball?"

"Exactly," Marcus chuckled, nudging Alex playfully. "And maybe I'll finally beat you at air hockey this time."

Alex grinned, accepting the challenge. "We'll see about that, Marcus. Let the games begin!"

"Challenge accepted," Marcus replied, a competitive glint in his eye. "But first, let's find a quieter corner to chat."

They weaved through the bustling arcade, eventually finding a secluded area with a couple of empty chairs tucked away from the main crowd.

"Here looks good," Marcus said, pulling out a chair and motioning for Alex to sit. "Alright, Alex, let's get down to business. I've been doing some serious thinking since our last encounter."

Alex settled into his seat, curious about Marcus's intentions. "Go on," he encouraged, leaning forward attentively.

Marcus took a deep breath before continuing. "I realized I let my ego get the best of me during the interview. We've been through too much together to let something like that tear us apart."

Alex nodded, appreciating Marcus's honesty. "I agree, Marcus. I've been reflecting on it too, and I don't want our friendship to suffer because of a silly disagreement."

"Good," Marcus said, a sense of relief evident in his voice. "Because at the end of the day, we're a team. And teams stick together, no matter what."

A smile tugged at the corners of Alex's lips. "Absolutely. So, where do we go from here?"

Marcus grinned, a sense of optimism returning to his expression. "Forward, as friends and allies. And maybe a few rounds of air hockey to celebrate?"

Alex chuckled, feeling a weight lift off his shoulders. "Sounds like a plan, Marcus. Let's do it."

They rose from their seats, ready to immerse themselves in the arcade's array of games.

"Alright, but just so you know, I'm not going easy on you," Alex teased, a competitive gleam in his eye.

"Bring it on," Marcus shot back, a playful smirk on his face as they headed towards the air hockey table.

The clack of the puck echoed in the air as they battled it out, their laughter mingling with the sounds of the arcade.

It was already morning, the day was busy as usual in the heart of London, there was a shadowy presence of some organization that loomed over the streets, it was called the "Hood", a notorious criminal organization, that held the metropolis in its grip, spreading fear and chaos with impunity as it carried out its nefarious deeds.

It was said that The Hood had risen from the ashes of a bygone era, its roots sinking deep into the underbelly of the city where corruption and crime festered unchecked. Over the years, it had grown in power and influence, its reach extending far beyond the confines of its humble beginnings.

At the helm of this criminal empire lurked a figure shrouded in mystery, known only as Mr Big—a shadowy mastermind who pulled the strings from behind the scenes, orchestrating elaborate schemes with ruthless efficiency.

But while Mr. Big remained hidden in the shadows, his presence was felt acutely throughout the city, his influence permeating every facet of daily life. From petty thefts and extortion rackets to large-scale heists and organized crime, The Hood's reach knew no bounds.

There is a shady Mayor (Mayor Cretin) who is letting the Hood, get away with the major crime wave that has hit London by being too lenient and making excuses for them and Lucas and his gang as low-level members feel untouchable and they get worse. Mayor Cretin, the city's elected leader, was well aware of The Hood's activities but chose to turn a blind eye to their atrocities in exchange for a hefty payoff. Under his watchful eye, the city had descended into lawlessness, with crime rates soaring to unprecedented levels.

Mayor Cretin, in his opulent office, his fingers tented beneath his chin as he gazed out at the skyline below. His appearance was as polished as his demeanour was deceitful, with a slicked-back mane of silver hair and a meticulously tailored suit that exuded an air of authority and refinement.

But behind the façade of respectability lay a man consumed by greed and ambition, his every decision driven by self-interest rather than the welfare of the city he purported to serve. Mayor Cretin had long ago sold his soul to the highest bidder, his allegiance bought and paid for by the shadowy figures who lurked in the corridors of power.

Mayor Cretin leaned back in his luxurious leather chair, his gaze lingering on the cityscape outside his window.

As he pondered his next move, a knock echoed through the room, and Mayor Cretin's trusted advisor entered, his obsequious smile firmly in place.

"Good evening, Mayor Cretin," the advisor greeted, his voice laced with deference. "I trust you're in good spirits tonight?"

Mayor Cretin nodded, though his expression remained inscrutable. "As good as can be expected, given the circumstances," he replied, his voice tinged with a hint of weariness. "But enough about me. Tell me, how are things progressing with our friends in The Hood?"

The advisor's smile faltered slightly, a shadow passing over his features.

"Well, Mayor Cretin, they continue to operate with... efficiency," he replied carefully, choosing his words with caution.

Mayor Cretin's eyes narrowed, a hint of impatience creeping into his voice. "Efficiency is all well and good, but what about results?" he demanded, his tone sharpening with each word. "Are they delivering on their end of the bargain?"

The advisor hesitated, acutely aware of the weight of Mayor Cretin's expectations. "There have been... complications," he admitted reluctantly, his gaze flickering to the floor.

Mayor Cretin's lips tightened into a thin line, his patience wearing thin. "Complications?" he repeated, his voice dangerously low. "What kind of complications?"

The advisor took a deep breath, steeling himself for what he was about to say. "Well, you see, Mayor Cretin, there have been reports of increased violence and unrest in the city," he explained, his voice trembling slightly. "It seems that The Hood's activities have become more... brazen, shall we say."

Mayor Cretin's expression darkened, a storm brewing behind his eyes.

"And what, pray tell, are you doing to rectify this situation?" he demanded, his voice sharp with anger.

The advisor shifted uncomfortably; "We're doing everything we can, Mayor Cretin," he assured hastily, his words coming out in a rush. "We've increased police presence in the affected areas, and we're working closely with law enforcement to bring the perpetrators to justice."

Mayor Cretin's gaze hardened, his disappointment palpable. "Bringing them to justice?" he scoffed, his voice dripping with disdain.

"Do you honestly expect me to believe that? You and I both know that justice is the last thing on your mind."

The advisor paled, the weight of Mayor Cretin's accusation settling heavily upon him. "Mayor Cretin, I assure you, we're doing everything in our power to address the situation," he protested, his voice trembling with fear.

But Mayor Cretin was unmoved, his eyes cold and unforgiving. "Your assurances mean nothing to me," he replied icily, his tone cutting like a knife. "I expect results, and if you can't deliver, then perhaps it's time I found someone who can."

The advisor swallowed hard, the gravity of Mayor Cretin's words sinking in. "I understand, Mayor Cretin," he murmured, his voice barely above a whisper. "I won't let you down again."

With a dismissive wave of his hand, Mayor Cretin turned his attention back to the window, his thoughts already drifting to his next move. For Mayor Cretin, power was everything, and he would stop at nothing to maintain his grip on it,

Lucas, a low-level member of The Hood, revelled in the chaos and anarchy that gripped the city. Alongside his gang of miscreants, he roamed the streets with impunity, his brazen acts of violence and intimidation striking fear into the hearts of the city's residents.

But while Lucas and his cronies basked in their power, Scarlette's boyfriend, Samuel, found himself torn between loyalty to his employer and his love for Scarlette. As the Mayor's trusted assistant, Samuel had been privy to the inner workings of City Hall, witnessing firsthand the extent of Mayor Cretin's corruption.

Scarlette couldn't shake off the feeling of unease that had settled in her heart regarding her relationship with Samuel. Despite his charming demeanour and successful career as the Mayor's assistant, Samuel's constant prioritization of work over their relationship had begun to take its toll. He often made promises he couldn't keep, leaving Scarlette feeling neglected and unimportant.

One evening, as they sat in a cosy cafe, Scarlette mustered up the courage to confront Samuel about his behaviour. "Samuel, I feel like we're drifting apart," she confessed, her voice tinged with sadness. "You're always so busy with work, and I don't feel like a priority in your life anymore."

Samuel sighed, running a hand through his hair in frustration. "I know, Scarlette, and I'm sorry," he replied, his eyes filled with remorse. "But you have to understand, my job is demanding, and I'm under a lot of pressure to perform well."

Despite his apology, Scarlette couldn't shake off the feeling of disappointment that lingered in her heart. She knew deep down that if things didn't change soon, she would have to make some difficult decisions about their relationship.

Meanwhile, Marcus found himself grappling with conflicting emotions as he watched Samuel and Scarlette's relationship unfold. He couldn't deny the pang of jealousy that surged through him every time he saw them together. He had harboured feelings for Scarlette for as long as he could remember, but he knew that pursuing her would only complicate their friendship.

One evening, as they all gathered at a mutual friend's party, Marcus found himself unable to contain his emotions any longer. He cornered Scarlette in the garden, his heart pounding in his chest as he prepared to confess his feelings.

"Scarlette, there's something I need to tell you," Marcus began, his voice trembling slightly. "I've always had feelings for you, and seeing you with Samuel…it's been hard for me."

Scarlette's eyes widened in surprise, her heart skipping a beat at Marcus's confession. She had never considered the possibility that he might feel the same way about her. "Marcus, I…I had no idea," she stammered, at a loss for words.

Their conversation was interrupted by the arrival of Alex, Alex couldn't help but notice the tension between them.

"Hey guys, what's going on?" Alex asked, shooting Marcus a questioning look.

Marcus quickly composed himself, plastering a fake smile on his face. "Oh, nothing, just catching up," he replied, shooting a meaningful glance at Scarlette.

As the days passed, Alex found himself slowly healing from the heartbreak caused by Breezy's betrayal. He threw himself into his studies, seeking solace in the familiar routine of school and the company of his friends.

One day, as he sat in the school library poring over his textbooks, a voice interrupted his thoughts. "Excuse me, is this seat taken?"

Alex looked up to find a girl standing before him, her eyes sparkling with warmth and kindness. She had a friendly smile on her face, and Alex couldn't help but be drawn to her gentle demeanour.

"Uh, no, it's not taken," Alex replied, gesturing to the empty seat opposite him.

The girl smiled gratefully and took a seat, introducing herself as Helen. She explained that she was new to the school and was looking for a quiet place to study.

As they struck up a conversation, Alex couldn't help but notice how effortlessly it flowed. Helen was easy to talk to, and soon they were discussing everything from their favourite subjects in school to their hobbies outside of class.

"So, what's your favourite subject?" Helen asked, flipping through one of Alex's textbooks with curiosity.

"Math," Alex replied with a small smile. "I know, it's not the most popular choice, but there's something about solving equations that just clicks with me. What about you?"

Helen chuckled softly. " I quite enjoy math too. But if I had to pick a favourite, it would probably be literature. There's just so much to explore in the world of words."

Their conversation meandered from topic to topic, seamlessly transitioning from school to personal interests. Alex learned that Helen had recently moved to the area due to her father's job and was still adjusting to the new school environment.

# CHAPTER THREE

## INVITATION TO THE PORTAL

"It must be tough being the new kid," Alex remarked sympathetically.

Helen nodded a hint of wistfulness in her eyes. "It has its challenges, but meeting people like you makes it easier."

Alex felt a warm flutter in his chest at her words. He found himself opening up to Helen in a way he hadn't with many others. Before he knew it, hours had passed, and the library was closing for the day.

As they gathered their belongings to leave, Alex couldn't shake the feeling of excitement that bubbled within him. Meeting Helen had been unexpected, but he couldn't deny the connection he felt with her

"Hey, do you want to grab a coffee or something sometime?" Alex blurted out before he could stop himself, his heart pounding with anticipation.

Helen's eyes lit up with a smile. "I'd love to! It would be nice to explore the area a bit more."

They exchanged contact information, making plans to meet up over the weekend. As they walked out of the library together, Alex couldn't help but feel a sense of excitement for the future.

Alex found himself captivated by Helen's intelligence and wit. They bonded over their shared love of literature and art, and before long, they had exchanged phone numbers and made plans to meet up after school.

Their first date was a whirlwind of laughter and conversation as they explored the city together, visiting museums and art galleries and sharing stories about their lives. Alex felt a sense of ease and comfort in Helen's presence as if he had known her for years rather than just a few hours.

But little did Alex know that their budding romance had caught the attention of someone from his past. Breezy, unable to let go of her feelings for Alex, had been keeping a close eye on him ever since their breakup. And when she saw him out with Helen, her jealousy flared up like wildfire.

Determined to win Alex back at any cost, Breezy resorted to desperate measures to sabotage his relationship with Helen. She followed them wherever they went, lurking in the shadows and plotting her next move.

But no matter how hard she tried, Breezy's attempts always failed. From accidentally spilling drinks on Helen to tripping over her own feet in a clumsy attempt to catch Alex's attention, Breezy's antics served to amuse Alex and Helen.

One evening, as they sat in a cosy cafe, Breezy mustered up the courage to confront Alex about his new relationship. "Alex, we need to talk," she said, her voice trembling with emotion.

Alex sighed, running a hand through his hair in frustration. "Breezy, I've told you before, it's over between us," he replied, his tone firm but gentle. "I've moved on, and so should you."

But Breezy refused to listen, her heart filled with resentment and bitterness. "You can't just throw away what we had," she pleaded, her eyes brimming with tears. "I made a mistake, but I still love you, Alex."

Alex shook his head, his heart heavy with sadness. "I'm sorry, Breezy, but I can't go back to how things were," he said, his voice tinged with regret. "I need to move forward with my life, and so do you."

As Breezy stormed out of the cafe, her tears mingling with the rain outside, Alex turned to Helen with a weary smile. "I'm sorry you had to see that," he said, his eyes filled with apology.

Helen reached out and took his hand in hers, her touch warm and comforting. "It's okay, Alex," she replied, her voice filled with understanding. "We'll get through this together."

And as they sat together in the dimly lit cafe, their fingers intertwined and their hearts entwined, Alex knew that he had found something special in Helen. She was more than just a rebound or a distraction – she was his guiding light in a world filled with darkness, his anchor in a sea of uncertainty.

As the echoes of Breezy's departure faded into the night, Alex, Marcus, and Scarlette found themselves standing in the dimly lit street the following day, the weight of their encounter still hanging heavy in the air. Scarlette turned to Alex, concern etched across her features. "Are you okay, Alex?" she asked, her voice soft with worry.

Alex nodded, forcing a weak smile. "I'll be fine," he replied, though his thoughts were still consumed by the tumultuous events that happened.

Marcus, ever the optimist, clapped Alex on the back with a grin. "Well, that was certainly eventful," he quipped, attempting to lighten the mood. "But hey, at least we got a good story out of it, right?"

Before Alex could respond, a soft humming sound filled the air, growing louder with each passing moment. Suddenly, a shimmering portal materialized before them, Out stepped Lyra, a fierce and hotheaded rogue who hailed from a realm of shadows. With her emerald eyes blazing with determination and her quick wit, she had a knack for infiltrating enemy camps and gathering vital information. Clad in armour reminiscent of ancient warriors, her blonde hair cascaded down her shoulders, giving her an almost ethereal appearance. At her side hung a sword, a symbol of her strength and prowess in battle, while a whip coiled around her waist, a tool she used not only as a weapon but also to swing effortlessly through the dense forest, showcasing her agility accompanied by her is Dippy, the living app who had become a trusted ally in their previous adventures.

"Lyra! Dippy!" Alex exclaimed, his surprise quickly giving way to excitement. "What are you doing here?"

Lyra smiled warmly, her eyes sparkling with determination. "We've come with urgent news from Esmeria," she explained, her voice grave. "There's a new threat looming, and we need your help."

Marcus's eyes widened with interest, his curiosity piqued. "A new threat?" he echoed, his voice tinged with excitement. "What kind of threat?"

Dippy, ever the eager informant, chimed in with a series of holographic images depicting the dangers facing Esmeria. "It appears that a powerful sorcerer has emerged, intent on unleashing chaos and destruction upon our world," he explained, his voice crackling with static.

Scarlette frowned, her brow furrowed in concern. "That sounds serious," she remarked, her voice filled with apprehension. "What can we do to help?"

Lyra turned to Alex, her gaze intense. "We need to gather our allies and prepare for battle," she said, her voice resolute. "But first, we must attend the Battle of Dimensions celebrations. It's a time-honoured tradition, where warriors from different realms come together to test their skills and forge new alliances."

Alex nodded, understanding the gravity of the situation. "We'll do whatever it takes to protect Esmeria," he vowed, his voice firm with determination. "Count us in."

Marcus grinned, his eyes shining with excitement. "You can count on us, Lyra," he declared, his voice brimming with confidence.

As Lyra and Dippy explained the urgency of the situation in Esmeria, Marcus couldn't help but find himself drawn to the Lyra. Her confidence, coupled with the air of mystery that surrounded her, captivated him in a way he couldn't quite explain.

Lost in his thoughts, Marcus barely noticed the subtle shift in Scarlette's demeanour beside him. Her eyes narrowed ever so slightly as she observed the way Marcus's gaze lingered on Lyra, a flicker of concern tugging at her heartstrings.

But Lyra remained oblivious to the brewing tension between her companions, her focus solely on the task at hand. "We need to act quickly," she insisted, her voice tinged with urgency. "Esmeria is in grave danger, and we cannot afford to delay."

Alex nodded in agreement, his expression grave. "We'll do everything in our power to help," he reassured her, determination blazing in his eyes.

Meanwhile, Marcus found himself torn between his growing admiration for Lyra and his lingering feelings for Scarlette. He had harboured a secret crush on Scarlette for quite some time, admiring her strength and resilience in the face of adversity.

Just then, Lyra turned to Alex and Marcus, her expression serious. "I need you both to be ready to join us in Esmeria at a moment's notice," she said her voice firm. "We'll be in touch as soon as we have a plan in place."

Marcus's heart skipped a beat at the prospect of accompanying Lyra to Esmeria, his excitement palpable. "You can count on us, Lyra," he declared a hint of eagerness in his voice.

With a final nod of farewell, Lyra and Dippy stepped through the shimmering portal, disappearing from view in an instant. And as the portal closed behind them.

As the shimmering portal closed behind Lyra and Dippy, leaving Alex, Marcus, and Scarlette standing in the quiet street, an air of anticipation hung in the air. Marcus's mind raced with conflicting emotions, torn between his growing attraction to Lyra and his longstanding feelings for Scarlette.

Scarlette glanced at Marcus, her heart heavy with uncertainty. She had noticed the way his gaze lingered on Lyra, a flicker of jealousy stirring in the depths of her soul. But she pushed aside her insecurities, knowing that they had a greater purpose to fulfill.

"We have to help them," Marcus declared suddenly, his voice breaking through the silence. "Esmeria is in danger, and we can't just sit back and do nothing."

Alex nodded in agreement, his expression grave. "You're right," he said, his voice tinged with determination. "We've faced countless challenges together, and this is no different. We stand with Esmeria."

Scarlette bit her lip, her heart swelling with pride at their unwavering resolve. "I'm with you," she affirmed, her voice steady despite the turmoil swirling inside her.

As they made their way back to their respective homes, Marcus's thoughts were consumed by visions of Esmeria and the mysterious sorcerer threatening its peace. But amidst the chaos, one thought lingered above all others – Lyra.

He couldn't shake the memory of her presence, the way her eyes sparkled with determination and her voice resonated with authority. Despite his feelings for Scarlette, there was something about Lyra that drew him in like a moth to a flame.

As the days passed, the group prepared for their journey to

Esmeria, gathering supplies and making arrangements for their departure. Marcus threw himself into the preparations with a newfound sense of purpose, his mind focused on the task at hand.

But as the day of their departure drew near, Marcus found himself increasingly preoccupied with thoughts of Lyra. Try as he might, he couldn't shake the feeling that she held the key to unlocking the mysteries of Esmeria – and perhaps his own heart.

It was a school hour, and the halls of the school buzzed with excitement as students hurried to their classes, their minds filled with the promise of another day of learning. But amidst the chatter and laughter, a sense of unease hung in the air – a foreboding shadow that threatened to darken the day's proceedings.

In the midst of it all, Alex made his way to his first-period class, his thoughts consumed by the events of the previous evening. The news of Mr. Ransford's arrest had spread like wildfire, sending shockwaves through the student body.

Mr. Ransford, the beloved headteacher and mentor to countless students, had been falsely accused of a heinous crime – embezzlement. The accusations came out of nowhere, seemingly orchestrated by unseen forces intent on silencing his outspoken criticism of the Mayor's alleged ties to The Hood.

As Alex entered the classroom, he found his classmates gathered in hushed groups, their faces drawn with worry. The atmosphere was tense, charged with an undercurrent of fear and suspicion.

Marcus approached Alex with a grim expression, his eyes dark with concern. "Have you heard the news?" he asked, his voice barely above a whisper.

Alex nodded solemnly, his heart heavy with sorrow. "I can't believe they arrested Mr. Ransford," he replied, his voice tinged with disbelief. "It's all just a setup to silence him."

Mr Ransford had also helped Alex and his friends in their battle against Ruok, in their first fight against the dark power.

Just then, the classroom door swung open, revealing a sombre-looking Mr Ransford flanked by two stern-faced police officers. The sight sent a ripple of shock through the room, the students falling silent as they watched their beloved teacher being escorted away like a common criminal.

"Mr. Ransford!" Alex called out, his voice filled with desperation. "We know you're innocent!"

But Mr. Ransford merely offered him a sad smile, his eyes reflecting the pain of betrayal. "Thank you, Alex," he said, his voice barely audible over the din of the classroom. "But right now, the truth doesn't seem to matter."

With that, he was gone, leaving behind a classroom full of stunned and outraged students.

As news of Mr. Ransford's arrest spread throughout the school, a wave of anger swept through the student body. Rumours swirled about the circumstances of his arrest – how he had been falsely accused based on flimsy evidence concocted by the Mayor's cronies.

It all began innocently enough, with Mr. Ransford's keen sense of justice and unwavering dedication to his students. As the headteacher of the school, he had always been a vocal advocate for the rights and well-being of the students under his care.

But as he noticed some wrongdoings in his city, he moved into the inner workings of the city, Mr. Ransford began to uncover a web of corruption and deceit that stretched far beyond the confines of the school walls. He witnessed firsthand the devastating impact of The Hood's criminal activities – the drugs, the violence, and the despair that gripped the city like a vice.

Determined to make a difference, Mr Ransford took a bold stand against The Hood, publicly condemning their actions and calling for an end to their reign of terror.

Mr. Ransford stood at the podium, his eyes scanning the faces of the crowd gathered before him. They looked to him with hope, seeking guidance in these tumultuous times.

"My friends," he began, his voice steady and resolute, "we find ourselves at a crossroads. The shadows of corruption loom large over our beloved town, moving a pall of fear and uncertainty upon us all."

A murmur of agreement rippled through the crowd, urging Mr. Ransford to continue.

"But fear not, for we are not alone in this fight," he declared, his words infused with conviction. "Together, we possess the power to bring about change, to challenge the status quo, and to dismantle the oppressive forces that seek to hold us captive."

The crowd nodded in solidarity, their eyes reflecting the flicker of hope ignited by Mr. Ransford's words.

"But let us not be content with mere words," he pressed on, his tone growing more impassioned. "It is not enough to simply decry the injustices that surround us. We must take action, bold and unyielding, in the face of adversity."

A swell of determination coursed through the crowd, fueling Mr. Ransford's resolve.

"For too long, we have turned a blind eye to the machinations of The Hood," he continued, his voice ringing out with righteous indignation. "But no more! The time has come for us to confront the truth, to shine a light into the darkest corners of our society."

A wave of agreement washed over the crowd, their voices rising in fervent agreement.

"And what of the Mayor?" Mr. Ransford challenged, his gaze piercing through the crowd. "Is he not complicit in the crimes perpetrated by The Hood? Does he not bear responsibility for the suffering inflicted upon our community?"

The crowd murmured in assent, their frustration with the Mayor's perceived negligence in the air.

"But fear not," Mr. Ransford reassured them, his voice tinged with defiance. "For we hold within us the power to hold him to account, to demand transparency, and to usher in a new era of governance founded upon integrity and justice."

A chorus of cheers erupted from the crowd, their spirits lifted by Mr Ransford's unwavering resolve.

"We are the architects of our destiny," he proclaimed, his voice echoing with the weight of certainty. "Together, we will tear down the walls of corruption and build a future worthy of our dreams!"

But his outspokenness didn't end there.

As he dug deeper, Mr Ransford uncovered disturbing evidence suggesting that the Mayor himself was complicit in The Hood's operations – turning a blind eye to their criminal activities in exchange for political favours and financial gain.

Armed with this damning evidence, Mr. Ransford became even more vocal in his criticism of the Mayor, openly accusing him of corruption and collusion with The Hood. His impassioned speeches and fiery rhetoric struck a chord with the community, rallying support for his cause and igniting a firestorm of controversy.

But his boldness came at a cost. The Mayor, feeling threatened by Mr. Ransford's accusations, retaliated with a vicious smear campaign aimed at discrediting him and silencing his dissent.

False rumours began to circulate, painting Mr Ransford as a dangerous radical hell-bent on undermining the city's stability. The Mayor's cronies seized upon these rumours, fabricating evidence of embezzlement to justify Mr Ransford's arrest and removal from his position of influence.

And so, Mr Ransford found himself falsely accused of a crime he did not commit – a pawn in the Mayor's ruthless quest for power and control. But even in the face of adversity, he refused to back down, his unwavering commitment to justice inspiring others to join the fight against corruption and injustice.

As he languished in jail, awaiting trial for a crime he knew he hadn't committed, Mr. Ransford found solace in the knowledge that his sacrifice had not been in vain. Even behind bars, his voice continued to ring out, a beacon of hope in a city shrouded in darkness.

The students rallied outside the imposing façade of the mayor's office, their voices raised in a chorus of defiance as they demanded justice for Mr. Ransford. They held homemade signs bearing slogans like "Free Ransford" and "End Corruption Now," their determination shining through despite the looming threat of arrest.

Alex, Marcus, and Scarlette stood at the forefront of the protest, their impassioned pleas echoing off the cold stone walls of the building. "Mr. Ransford is innocent!" Alex shouted, his voice ringing with conviction. "We won't rest until he's released!"

Marcus waved his sign high above his head, his eyes blazing with determination. "The Mayor can't silence us!" he declared, his voice carrying over the crowd. "We won't stop until justice is served!"

Scarlette joined in the chorus of voices, her words filled with righteous indignation. "We demand transparency!" she cried, her fists clenched in defiance. "We won't let the Mayor get away with this!"

But their peaceful protest soon turned chaotic as the Mayor's supporters descended upon them, intent on quelling the uprising by any means necessary. The air crackled with tension as the two groups clashed, fists flying and insults hurled.

Amidst the chaos, the police arrived in force, their presence a stark reminder of the consequences of defying authority. "Disperse immediately or face arrest!" they bellowed, their voices booming over the tumult.

Some of the students heeded the warning and began to scatter, but others stood their ground, unwilling to back down in the face of intimidation. Alex, Marcus, and Scarlette remained steadfast, their resolve unshaken by the looming threat of arrest.

But as the police moved in to make arrests, chaos erupted once more. Some students were dragged away kicking and screaming, their pleas for mercy falling on deaf ears. Others were forcibly restrained, their hands bound with zip ties as they were led away in handcuffs.

Alex watched in horror as his classmates were taken into custody, his heart heavy with guilt for dragging them into the fight for justice. "I'm sorry," he whispered, his voice barely audible over the din. "I never meant for any of this to happen."

But even as the arrests were made, the protest continued unabated. The remaining students refused to be silenced, their voices ringing out in defiance against the injustices that plagued their community.

Hours passed as the standoff continued, both sides unwilling to back down. But eventually, the tide began to turn as word spread of the students' plight.

The school committee, outraged by the heavy-handed tactics employed by the police, intervened on behalf of the students, demanding their immediate release and an investigation into the events that had transpired.

After much negotiation and deliberation, the students were finally released from custody, their spirits battered but unbroken. They emerged from the ordeal with a renewed sense of purpose, their resolve strengthened by their brush with injustice.

As they returned to the school grounds, they were met with a hero's welcome, their classmates cheering and applauding their bravery in the face of adversity. For in their fight for justice, they had become symbols of hope and resilience, shining beacons of light in a city shrouded in darkness.

It was a crisp autumn evening when Scarlette stumbled upon the truth that would shatter her world into a million pieces. She had grown suspicious of her boyfriend's late-night meetings and secretive phone calls, but it wasn't until she accidentally stumbled upon a hidden folder on his laptop that the full extent of his betrayal became clear.

# CHAPTER FOUR

## BETRAYAL UNVEILED

As she clicked through the files, her heart sank like a stone in her chest. Documents detailing illicit deals, money laundering schemes, and clandestine meetings with known members of The Hood littered the screen before her eyes. And at the centre of it all was her boyfriend, his face twisted in a smirk of greed and deceit.

As Scarlette clicked through the files in the hidden folder on her boyfriend's laptop, her heart pounded in her chest with a mixture of dread and disbelief. Each document she opened revealed another layer of deception and corruption, painting a damning picture of her boyfriend's involvement with The Hood and the Mayor.

The first file she opened was labelled "Financial Transactions." Inside, she found spreadsheets detailing large sums of money being transferred between various accounts, all linked back to her boyfriend's name. The figures were staggering, indicating a pattern of illicit financial activity that could only be explained by involvement in criminal enterprises.

Scarlette's hands trembled as she clicked on the next file, labelled "Meeting Notes." It contained detailed records of clandestine meetings held in dimly lit backrooms and secluded alleyways, the participants identified only by code names and initials. As she read through the notes, Scarlette's stomach churned with disgust at the brazenness of their discussions and the lengths they were willing to go to further their nefarious agenda.

But perhaps the most incriminating file of all was labelled simply "Evidence." Scarlette hesitated for a moment before opening it, her heart pounding in her chest with a mixture of dread and determination. Inside, she found a trove of photographs, audio recordings, and video footage documenting her boyfriend's dealings with known members of The Hood and the Mayor himself.

As she scrolled through the damning evidence, Scarlette felt a surge of anger and betrayal wash over her.

In a state of shock and disbelief, Scarlette confronted her boyfriend with the evidence she had uncovered, her voice trembling with anger and hurt. "How could you do this to me?" she demanded, her eyes flashing with righteous indignation. "Do you have any idea what you've done?"

But her boyfriend merely laughed, his expression twisted in a smirk of arrogance. "It's just business, Scarlette," he replied dismissively. "You wouldn't understand."

Scarlette's blood boiled at his callous words, her hands balling into fists at her sides. "You've betrayed everything we had together," she spat, her voice dripping with venom. "I won't be a part of your criminal enterprise any longer."

With a heavy heart, Scarlette made the difficult decision to end their relationship then and there, unwilling to be complicit in her boyfriend's crimes any longer.

As she turned to leave, her ex-boyfriend's demeanour shifted from indifference to outright hostility. "You can't walk away from this, Scarlette," he snarled, his eyes flashing with malice. "You know too much."

Before she could react, he lunged at her, his hands closing around her throat in a vice-like grip. Scarlette fought back with all her strength, her survival instincts kicking into overdrive as she struggled to break free from his grasp.

In a desperate bid for freedom, Scarlette managed to break free from his grip and fled into the night, her heart pounding in her chest with fear and adrenaline. She ran until her lungs burned and her legs threatened to give out beneath her, her mind racing with thoughts of what to do next.

It was then that she remembered Alex and Marcus, her trusted friends and allies in the fight against corruption and injustice. With no one else to turn to, she sought refuge in their company, her words tumbling out in a rush as she recounted the harrowing ordeal she had just endured.

"They tried to kill me, Alex," she gasped, her voice trembling with fear. "My ex-boyfriend and the Mayor – they're working with The Hood to get rich. And now they'll stop at nothing to silence me."

Alex and Marcus listened intently to Scarlette's story, their faces grim with determination. "We won't let them get away with this," Alex declared, his voice firm with resolve. "We'll expose them for the criminals they are and put an end to their reign of terror once and for all."

As Scarlette recounted her harrowing encounter with Samuel and the Mayor to Alex and Marcus, their expressions shifted from shock to concern as she detailed the betrayal and the attempt on her life, their anger simmering beneath the surface as they absorbed the gravity of the situation.

"I can't believe they would stoop so low," Marcus exclaimed, his fists clenched in frustration. "We have to do something about this."

Alex nodded in agreement, his mind already racing with plans for their next move. "We can't let them get away with this," he declared, his voice tinged with determination. "We need to expose them for the criminals they are."

Scarlette felt a surge of gratitude wash over her as she looked at her friends, their unwavering support giving her strength in the face of adversity. "Thank you," she whispered, her voice choked with emotion. "I don't know what I would do without you both. "However, now that the Mayor and Samuel are onto you, we may need to lay low. We can head to Esmeria for the Battle of Dimensions event and focus on our mission there" Alex replied. "Yay!" shouted Marcus excitedly. "It sounds fun and I've missed Esmeria! I can't wait to get my grubby hands on those Esmerian treats too!" They all laughed.

And so, with their decision made, the trio made their way to Alex's house to prepare for their journey to Esmeria. As they entered the familiar surroundings of Alex's home, they were greeted by the comforting warmth of family and familiarity.

Alex wasted no time in retrieving his ancient book from Vesta, eager to embark on their adventure to Esmeria. But as he rifled through his belongings, his excitement turned to dismay as he realized that the book was nowhere to be found.

"I can't believe I've lost it," he muttered, his face flushing with embarrassment. "It's the key to everything."

As Alex, Scarlette, and Marcus realized that the ancient book was nowhere to be found, a sense of panic threatened to overwhelm them. They knew that the book was crucial to their journey to Esmeria, and without it, their plans were in jeopardy.

But Alex refused to give up hope. "There must be another way," he declared, his voice tinged with determination. "We can't let this setback stop us."

Suddenly, a spark of memory ignited in Alex's mind as he recalled his first visit to Esmeria. It was during that journey that he stumbled upon the abandoned London Underground tunnel with the roller coaster trains to lead to the mystical realm.

"I remember something," Alex exclaimed, his eyes brightening with realization. "During my first visit to Esmeria, I discovered a hidden path – an abandoned London Underground tunnel that leads to Esmeria. We can use that to get there."

Scarlette and Marcus exchanged a glance, their curiosity piqued by Alex's revelation. "Are you sure about this, Alex?" Scarlette asked, her voice filled with uncertainty.

Alex nodded confidently. "Positive," he replied, his conviction unwavering. "It's our best chance of getting to Esmeria without the ancient book."

With their decision made, the trio set out in search of the hidden path to the abandoned London Underground tunnel. They retraced Alex's steps from his first visit to Esmeria, roaming through the busy streets of London with a sense of purpose and determination. As they approached the entrance to the underground tunnel, a sense of apprehension washed over them. The tunnel was dark and foreboding, its entrance shrouded in shadows as if concealing secrets of centuries past.

Abandoned roller coaster tracks snaked through the space, their rusted frames carrying roller coaster trains but these weren't ordinary roller coasters; Marcus and Scarlette were surprised, they were unlike anything he had ever seen. They remember the first time they travelled there, was through the magical book Vesta, the Queen of the underworld gave Alex. They seemed to shimmer with an otherworldly energy. Marcus and Scarlette's eyes widened as they realized that each roller coaster train was heading toward a different portal, each labelled with a different destination. And one of those portals bore the name "Esmeria."

The portal labelled "Esmeira" beckoned to him like a doorway to another realm, a realm that held the promise of adventure and answers to the questions that had been swirling in his mind.

Marcus and Scarlette hesitated for only a moment before

curiosity and a sense of urgency propelled them forward. With a deep breath, they all stepped off the platform onto the roller coaster train and strapped themselves in their seat. "Esmeria, here we come!" Marcus said excitedly and the train as if obeying his command, shot off like a bullet with Alex feeling a tingling sensation wash over him as he crossed the threshold of the portal.

In an instant, the world around him transformed. Colours danced and swirled, and he felt as if he was being pulled through a tunnel of shimmering light.

When they opened his eyes again, they found themselves in a place that defied description. The air was charged with otherworldly energy, and the landscape was a surreal blend of vibrant colours and unfamiliar structures.

The train then slowed down and stopped at a platform that was suspended in mid-air, overlooking a breathtaking expanse that stretched into the distance. They stepped onto the platform and before them, a sprawling city emerged its architecture was a fusion of futuristic designs and fantastical elements. Towers of glass and metal reached for the sky, adorned with intricate patterns and earning an ethereal glow. Bridges arched gracefully between buildings, and colossal sculptures seemed to defy gravity.

Alex's heart raced as he took in the sight before him. He was in Esmeira, a world beyond his wildest imagination. The roller coaster tracks continued from where he stood, weaving through the city like a network of veins, inviting him to explore further.

But Alex led the way, his determination driving them forward. With each step they took, the air grew colder and the sound of their footsteps echoed off the walls of the tunnel.

As Marcus, Alex, and Scarlette stepped through the portal into Esmeria, they were immediately struck by the breathtaking beauty and wonder of their surroundings. The air was alive with magic, swirling around them in a kaleidoscope of colours and sensations.

Marcus, ever the vigilant guardian, surveyed their new surroundings with a sense of awe and determination. His eyes narrowed as he took in the sights before him, his senses alert for any signs of danger. He quickly remembered they'd been there before.

"By the stars," Marcus breathed, his voice filled with wonder. "I've never seen anything like this before. It's... incredible." The last time we came here I didn't notice something like this.

"This is amazing!" Alex exclaimed; his voice tinged with exhilaration. "I feel like a kid in a candy store! Look at that!" he pointed eagerly at a group of shimmering faeries flitting through the air, leaving trails of glittering light in their wake.

Scarlette, with her quick wit and sharp tongue, was quick to add her observations to the mix. She surveyed their new surroundings with a critical eye, taking note of the subtle nuances and quirks that set Esmeria apart from their world.

"Well, this is certainly... different from what we saw the last time we came, probably because we used another passage channel to enter here then," Scarlette remarked dryly, her lips quirking into a wry smile. "I've seen some strange things in my time, but this takes the cake."

Marcus was captivated by the majestic creatures that roamed the land, though he had seen some of them before on their first visit to Esmeria.

"I've never seen anything like it," Marcus murmured, his voice filled with reverence. "These creatures... they're like something out of a dream."

Alex, meanwhile, found himself drawn to the vibrant flora and fauna that adorned Esmeria's forests and meadows. He ran his fingers along the petals of a luminescent flower, marvelling at its delicate beauty.

"I've always loved nature," Alex confessed, his eyes shining with admiration. "But this... this is something else entirely. It's like stepping into a painting."

Scarlette, ever the pragmatist, remained sceptical of their new surroundings, her sharp eyes scanning the surroundings for any signs of trouble. Yet even she couldn't help but be drawn in by the sheer spectacle of Esmeria's landscape.

"I'll admit, it's impressive," Scarlette conceded, her tone begrudgingly admiring. "But let's not forget why we're here. We have a job to do, remember?"

And so, with their initial awe and wonder tempered by a sense of purpose and determination, Marcus, Alex, and Scarlette set out to uncover the mysteries of Esmeria and fulfil their destiny in this strange and wondrous land.

As Marcus, Alex Knight, and Scarlette journeyed into the Esmeria, they found themselves in an ethereal mist that seemed to shimmer and dance around them. The air was alive with magic, humming with an energy that pulsed through their veins.

Suddenly, from the depths of the forest, a figure emerged – a majestic creature unlike any they had ever seen. It stood tall and proud, with shimmering silver fur that caught the light of the setting sun. Its eyes glowed with an otherworldly brilliance, and its presence exuded an aura of power and wisdom.

"What... what is that?" Marcus whispered, his voice barely audible above the rustle of the leaves. His hand instinctively went to the hilt of his D-blaster they took along with them to Esmeria, ready to defend his companions if need be.

Alex Knight, ever the curious, stepped forward with a sense of wonder. "I don't know, but it's beautiful," he murmured, his eyes wide with awe. "I've never seen anything like it."

Scarlette, with her keen sense of intuition, studied the creature with a mixture of caution and fascination. "It seems... friendly," she observed, her voice tinged with uncertainty. "But we should proceed with caution."

As they approached the creature, it lowered its head in a gesture of greeting, its eyes filled with warmth and understanding. In a voice that seemed to resonate from deep within their souls, she spoke:

"Fear not, young ones, for I mean you no harm. I am Silvoria, guardian of the ancient forest and servant to Queen Vesta, overseer of the world."

Marcus, ever the vigilant protector, eyed Silvoria with a mixture of scepticism and respect. "Queen Vesta? How did she know we've arrived already? Well…. she was the one that invited us for a celebration, does she want to see us now ?"

Silvoria's gaze softened, and she inclined her head in acknowledgement. "Her Majesty awaits you, brave adventurers. She has sensed the stirring of destiny in your hearts and wishes to speak with you."

Alex Knight's answered, "Us? But why?"

Silvoria's expression grew solemn. "All will be revealed in due time, young one.

Scarlette, always quick to read between the lines, sensed a deeper meaning behind Silvoria's words. "What kind of challenges?" she pressed; her voice laced with determination.

Silvoria's eyes glinted with an otherworldly wisdom. "That is for you to discover, my dear. But know that you are not alone. The fate of Esmeria – and perhaps even your world – rests in your hands."

With that, Silvoria turned and began to lead the way into the forest, her graceful movements guiding them like a beacon of hope in the gathering darkness.

As they followed Silvoria through the ancient trees, Marcus, Alex Knight, and Scarlette exchanged glances, as they were greeted by a jubilant crowd, Queen Vest, the overseer of the world of Esmeira herself, stood at the forefront, her regal presence commanding attention as she welcomed the newcomers with open arms.

"Welcome back once again to the realm of Esmeria!" Queen Vesta's voice echoed through the air, her tone warm and inviting. Her eyes sparkled with a combination of wisdom and kindness as she addressed the group. "It is an honour to have guests from afar join us for 'The Battle of Dimensions' celebration." Though they were here before it had been a while since they left us.

Alex and his friends exchanged glances, each feeling a sense of awe at being personally welcomed by the queen of Esmeria. The name of the celebration alone stirred their curiosity, hinting at the grandeur and excitement that awaited them.

"We extend our deepest gratitude to you for gracing us with your presence," Queen Vesta continued, her voice carrying a hint of reverence. "The Battle of Dimensions is a time of great significance in Esmerian history—a time when we come together to celebrate the unity and diversity of our realm."

Marcus, always the vigilant protector, nodded respectfully in response. "Thank you, Your Majesty," he said, his voice steady with respect. "We are humbled by your hospitality and honoured to be a part of such a momentous occasion."

Queen Vesta smiled warmly at Marcus's words, her eyes filled with a mixture of admiration and gratitude. "The honour is ours, brave guardian," she replied, her voice soft but filled with authority. "Your presence brings strength and courage to our realm, and for that, we are truly grateful."

Lyra, unable to contain her excitement, stepped forward with a grin. "We've heard tales of Esmeria's wonders and adventures," she exclaimed, her eyes shining with anticipation. "To be here and experience it firsthand is beyond anything we could have imagined!"

Scarlette, ever the pragmatist, observed the queen with a keen eye, taking note of her every word and gesture. "Forgive our ignorance, Your Majesty," she interjected, her tone respectful but curious. "But could you enlighten us further on the significance of 'The Battle of Dimensions'?"

Queen Vesta's smile widened at Scarlette's question, her gaze holding a hint of mystery. "Ah, 'The Battle of Dimensions' is more than just a celebration—it is a symbol of our resilience and unity," she explained, her voice carrying a sense of pride. "It commemorates the harmonious coexistence of our realm with others, as well as our ongoing quest for peace and understanding."

Alex nodded thoughtfully, absorbing Queen Vesta's words with appreciation for the depth of Esmerian culture and tradition. "It sounds like an incredible event," he remarked, his voice filled with genuine admiration. "We're honoured to be a part of it."

Queen Vesta inclined her head graciously in response, her eyes shining with warmth and appreciation. "As are we, young adventurer," she said, her voice tinged with a sense of anticipation. "May 'The Battle of Dimensions' bring you joy and unforgettable memories."

With that, Queen Vesta extended her hand in welcome, inviting Alex and his friends to join in the festivities and embark on a journey they would never forget.

As they made their way through the streets, they also got to the otherworldly theme park, they were greeted by a myriad of sights and sounds that dazzled the senses. Colourful banners fluttered in the breeze, announcing the various attractions and festivities taking place throughout the day.

Alex's eyes lit up with excitement as he caught sight of a towering roller coaster, its tracks twisting and turning through the air like a serpent in flight. "Now that looks like fun!" he exclaimed, his voice filled with enthusiasm.

Lyra, always the adventurous spirit, eagerly agreed. "I've always wanted to try one of those! Let's go!" she cried, already dragging Alex along in her wake.

# CHAPTER FIVE

## ADVENTURE AT THE THEME PARK: JOURNEY OF THRILLS AND WONDER

Marcus and Scarlette followed close behind, their expressions a mixture of amusement and apprehension. While they may have been reluctant at first, the infectious energy of the crowd soon had them joining in on the festivities with equal fervour.

As they waited in line for the roller coaster, they couldn't help but marvel at the ingenuity of Esmerian engineering. The ride itself was a masterpiece of design, with twists and turns that promised to exhilarate even the bravest of souls.

Finally, it was their turn to board the roller coaster, and as they strapped themselves in, a sense of exhilaration washed over them. The ride was a blur of adrenaline and excitement, with screams of joy mingling with the roar of the wind as they soared through the air.

As the group exited the roller coaster, their laughter and exhilaration filled the air. They walked through the theme park, soaking in the vibrant atmosphere and contemplating their next adventure.

Lyra grinned at Alex, her eyes sparkling with excitement. "That was amazing! I can't believe we finally tried it!"

Alex nodded enthusiastically, still buzzing from the adrenaline rush. "Yeah, that was insane! I've never felt so alive!"

Marcus chuckled, shaking his head in amusement. "You two certainly have a knack for seeking out excitement."

Scarlette smiled, her gaze wandering over the various attractions around them. "Well, isn't that what makes life interesting? Taking risks and experiencing new things?"

A nearby vendor caught their attention, offering a variety of treats and snacks. As they indulged in some delicious treats, they discussed their favourite moments from the roller coaster ride.

"I think my favourite part was when we went into that loop-the-loop!" Alex exclaimed, his eyes gleaming with excitement.

Lyra nodded in agreement. "Yeah, that was pretty epic! But I loved the moment right before the big drop. The anticipation was electrifying!"

Marcus chuckled, recalling how he had braced himself for the sudden plunge. "I must admit, I had my doubts at first, but that was worth it."

Scarlette nodded, savouring the sweet taste of her treat. "It's moments like these that make all the challenges we face worth it. We should make more time for adventures like this."

As they wandered through the park, they stumbled upon a whimsical Stellar Odyssey, As the group approached the entrance to Stellar Odyssey, they couldn't help but marvel at the sight before them. The towering structure loomed overhead, its sleek, futuristic design exuding an air of mystery and excitement.

"Whoa, this looks even cooler up close!" exclaimed Alex, his eyes alight with excitement.

Lyra nodded in agreement, a grin spreading across her face. "I can't wait to see what this ride has in store for us."

Marcus glanced around, taking in the bustling atmosphere of the park. "I've heard rumors about Stellar Odyssey. They say it's like nothing else out there."

Scarlette's heart raced with anticipation as they joined the queue, the hum of excitement palpable in the air. "Well, there's only one way to find out. Let's dive in and see for ourselves!"

As they reached the front of the line, they were greeted by a guide dressed in sleek, futuristic attire.

"Welcome, travelers, to Stellar Odyssey," the guide said with a warm smile. "Are you ready to embark on a journey through the cosmos?"

Alex nodded eagerly, his eyes shining with anticipation. "You bet we are! Let's do this."

The guide chuckled, motioning for them to follow. "Right this way, then. Please take your seats and prepare for departure."

The group followed the guide into the heart of the ride, where they were met with a dazzling array of seats arranged in a circular formation around a central console.

"These seats look comfy," remarked Lyra, sinking into her chair with a satisfied sigh.

Marcus nodded in agreement, adjusting his seatbelt with practiced ease. "Definitely beats waiting in line at the grocery store."

As they settled into their seats, the hum of the machinery around them grew louder, signaling that the ride was about to begin.

"Here we go!" exclaimed Scarlette, her heart pounding with excitement.

With a sudden surge of acceleration, Stellar Odyssey sprang to life. Lights flickered to life around them, casting the interior of the ride in a kaleidoscope of colors. The console in the center of the chamber hummed with energy as it powered up, ready to guide them on their cosmic adventure.

"Whoa, this is amazing!" cried Alex, his voice barely audible over the roar of the engines.

The guide nodded, a smile playing at the corners of their lips. "Hold on tight, travellers. Our journey through the stars is about to begin."

As Stellar Odyssey launched into the depths of space, they were plunged into a whirlwind of sights and sounds unlike anything they had ever experienced. Stars streaked past them in a blur of light as they soared deeper into the cosmos, the vastness of space stretching out before them in all its breathtaking splendor.

"I feel like I'm in a movie!" exclaimed Lyra, her eyes wide with wonder as they rocketed through the void of space.

Marcus laughed, his heart pounding with exhilaration. "This is even better than I imagined!"

As Stellar Odyssey continued its journey through the cosmos, they marveled at the wonders that unfolded before them. They sailed past distant planets and glittering asteroids, their senses overwhelmed by the sheer scale and beauty of the universe.

Hours seemed to pass in the blink of an eye as they traversed the vast expanse of space, each moment filled with awe and wonder. But eventually, as the ride began to slow, they knew that their cosmic adventure was drawing to a close.

With a final burst of energy, Stellar Odyssey returned to its berth, gently touching down as if guided by an unseen hand. The doors of the ride opened, and the group stepped out into the daylight, their minds still reeling from the incredible journey they had just undertaken.

As they made their way out of the ride, they couldn't help but feel a sense of gratitude for the opportunity to experience something truly extraordinary. And as they looked out at the world around them, they knew that they would carry the memories of their stellar odyssey with them always.

As they wandered through the park, their eyes alighted on a peculiar structure. It was unlike anything they had ever seen before.

"What in the world is that?" exclaimed Alex, pointing towards the strange contraption.

"Wow, what do you think this is?" wondered Alex, his eyes scanning the strange contraption.

Lyra shrugged, her curiosity piqued. "I have no idea, but it looks like it's going to be an adventure."

Marcus nodded in agreement, his gaze fixed on the swirling patterns adorning the ride. "Well, there's only one way to find out. Let's go check it out!"

As they approached the attraction, they were greeted by a sign that read "Time Warp" in bold, futuristic lettering. Without hesitation, they joined the queue, eager to uncover the secrets that lay within.

"Time Warp, huh?" mused Scarlette, glancing up at the mesmerizing lights. "Sounds like we're in for a wild ride."

The group exchanged excited glances, their hearts racing with anticipation. This was unlike anything they had ever experienced before, and they couldn't wait to see what awaited them on this thrilling adventure.

As they reached the front of the line, they were greeted by a guide dressed in colorful attire, their eyes twinkling with mischief.

"Welcome, brave travelers, to Time Warp!" exclaimed the guide, their voice filled with excitement. "Prepare to embark on a journey through time and space, where the laws of reality are mere suggestions."

Alex's eyes widened with excitement as he turned to his friends. "Did you hear that? We're going on a journey through time and space!"

Lyra grinned, her heart pounding with anticipation. "I can't wait to see where this ride takes us."

The guide led them into the heart of the attraction, where they were met with a dazzling array of seats arranged in a circular formation around a central console.

"These seats look so futuristic," remarked Marcus, running his hand over the sleek design.

As they settled into their seats and fastened their seatbelts, the hum of the machinery around them grew louder, signaling that the ride was about to begin.

"Here we go!" cried Scarlette, her excitement palpable.

With a sudden surge of acceleration, Time Warp sprang to life. Lights flickered to life around them, The console in the center of the chamber hummed with energy as it powered up, ready to guide them on their cosmic adventure.

As the ride launched into the depths of time and space, they were plunged into a whirlwind of sights and sounds unlike anything they had ever experienced. They soared through ancient civilizations and distant futures, their senses overwhelmed by the sheer scale and beauty of the universe.

"This is incredible!" exclaimed Alex, his voice barely audible over the roar of the engines.

Lyra laughed, her eyes shining with excitement. "I feel like we're on the adventure of a lifetime!"

"I feel like we're traveling through the pages of history," exclaimed Alex, his eyes wide with wonder as they hurtled through time and space.

Lyra laughed, her voice filled with excitement. "I never thought I'd get to witness the birth of the universe firsthand!"

As Time Warp continued its journey through the cosmos, they marveled at the wonders before them. They sailed past distant planets and shimmering stars, their hearts filled with a sense of awe and wonder.

Hours seemed to pass in the blink of an eye as they traversed the vast expanse of time and space, each moment filled with excitement and adventure, as the ride began to slow, they knew that their journey was drawing to a close.

With a final burst of energy, Time Warp returned to its berth, gently touching down as if guided by an unseen hand. The doors of the ride opened, and the group stepped out into the daylight, their minds still reeling from the incredible journey they had just undertaken.

As they made their way out of the ride, they couldn't help but feel a sense of exhilaration.

"This is incredible!" Lyra exclaimed, her eyes wide with wonder as they rose higher and higher into the sky.

Alex grinned, his adrenaline pumping as they reached the peak of their ascent. "I've never experienced anything like this before! It's like we're soaring among the stars!"

Marcus nodded, his senses tingling with the thrill of the ride. "It just goes to show, there's always something new and unexpected waiting to be discovered in this extraordinary realm."

they wandered further into the depths of the theme park, eager to explore more of its fantastical offerings. They stumbled upon the "Labyrinth of Illusions," a maze-like structure filled with optical illusions and mind-bending puzzles that challenged their perceptions of reality.

With each twist and turn, they found themselves transported to strange and surreal worlds, where up was down and left was right. It was a dizzying experience that left them questioning everything they thought they knew about the nature of existence.

Emerging from the labyrinth, they stumbled upon the "Whirlwind Whirlpool," a swirling vortex of energy that promised to whisk them away to distant dimensions. With a mixture of excitement and trepidation, they stepped into the swirling maelstrom, feeling the pull of unseen forces tugging at their very souls.

For what felt like an eternity, they were lost in a whirlwind of colors and sensations, hurtling through space and time with reckless abandon. It was a journey unlike any other, one that tested their courage and resolve to the very limit.

As they finally emerged from the whirlpool, breathless and exhilarated, they knew that they had experienced something truly extraordinary. In this otherworldly theme park, the boundaries of reality were blurred, and the possibilities were endless.

With their hearts full of wonder and excitement, they continued their journey through the park, eager to discover what other marvels awaited them in this enchanted realm. Little did they know that their adventure was only just beginning... As the capsule began its descent back to the ground, the group exchanged wide-eyed glances, still caught in the spell of the breathtaking experience they had just shared. Marcus leaned forward, his voice filled with awe. "That was truly remarkable, wasn't it? I feel like we've glimpsed a sliver of the universe's secrets."

Scarlette nodded, a sense of wonder evident in her eyes. "Absolutely! It's moments like these that remind us of the boundless wonders that exist beyond our everyday lives."

Lyra's hair shimmered in the soft glow of the descending capsule's lights, her voice carrying a hint of wistfulness. "I wish we could stay up there forever, surrounded by the stars and the endless expanse of the cosmos."

Alex smiled, his gaze lingering on the mesmerizing view outside the capsule's windows. "Perhaps one day we will, Lyra. But for now, let's cherish the memories we've made and carry them with us on our journey."

As they reached the ground and stepped out of the capsule, they found themselves in a tranquil clearing surrounded by lush greenery and colorful flowers. The air was filled with the sweet scent of blossoms, and a gentle breeze whispered through the trees, carrying with it the promise of new adventures.

In the center of the clearing stood a magnificent tree, its branches reaching towards the sky in a graceful dance. It seemed to pulse with life, emanating a warm and welcoming energy that enveloped them like a comforting embrace.

As they approached the tree, they felt a sense of peace wash over them, as if they had stumbled upon a sanctuary hidden away from the cares of the world. Marcus reached out to touch the rough bark, his fingertips tingling with a strange sensation.

"It's as if this tree holds the wisdom of the ages," he murmured, his voice barely above a whisper.

Scarlette nodded, her eyes shining with reverence. "I feel it too, Marcus. It's as if we've stumbled upon a sacred place, a refuge from the chaos and uncertainty of our lives."

Lyra stepped forward, her expression serene. "Perhaps this is what we've been searching for all along, a place where we can reconnect with the magic and wonder that lies within us."

Alex smiled, a sense of peace settling over him like a warm blanket. "Whatever it is, I'm grateful that we found it together. This moment, right here, feels like a gift—one that I will treasure always."

With their hearts full of gratitude and wonder, the group lingered beneath the branches of the magnificent tree, their souls nourished by the beauty and tranquility of the moment. As they prepared to leave the otherworldly realm behind and return to their ordinary lives, they carried with them the memories of their extraordinary adventure, knowing that they would forever be changed by the magic they had experienced.

As they strolled through the park, they stumbled upon a quaint little booth adorned with colourful flags and a sign that read

"Fortune Teller." Intrigued, they exchanged curious glances before Lyra spoke up.

"Hey, why don't we try this? It could be fun to see what the future holds," she suggested with a mischievous twinkle in her eye.

Alex shrugged, his curiosity piqued. "Sure, why not? It's all in good fun, right?"

Marcus and Scarlette exchanged amused smiles before nodding in agreement. "Let's give it a try," Marcus said, his tone tinged with scepticism.

They entered the booth and were greeted by a mysterious figure cloaked in robes, their face hidden beneath a veil. The fortune teller gestured for them to sit down, and they complied, their excitement building with each passing moment.

The fortune teller began to shuffle a deck of ancient-looking cards, their movements deliberate and precise. With a flourish, they laid out the cards in an intricate pattern, their expression unreadable.

As they studied the cards, the fortune teller began to speak in a voice that seemed to echo with wisdom and mystery. "Welcome, travellers, to the realm of fate and destiny. Let us peer into the veils of time and uncover the secrets that lie ahead."

Lyra leaned forward, her eyes wide with anticipation. "What do you see? What does the future hold for us?"

The fortune teller remained silent for a moment, their gaze

fixed on the cards before them. Finally, they spoke in a voice filled with cryptic wisdom. "I see journeys yet to be taken, challenges yet to be faced, and triumphs yet to be won. But remember, the future is not set in stone. It is shaped by the choices we make and the paths we choose to follow."

Alex exchanged a glance with his friends, a sense of wonder and excitement filling his heart. "That's both thrilling and mysterious. I guess we'll just have to wait and see what lies ahead."

As they left the booth, the group couldn't help but ponder the fortune teller's words, wondering what adventures and surprises awaited them on their journey.

While discussing the future they stumbled upon a stage where a lively performance was about to begin. A group of dancers adorned in colourful costumes stood ready to entertain the crowd with their vibrant routines.

Lyra's eyes lit up with excitement as she watched the dancers prepare. "Oh, this looks like it's going to be amazing! Let's find a good spot to watch!"

Alex nodded eagerly, already scanning the area for the perfect vantage point. "Agreed! I can't wait to see what they have in store for us."

Marcus and Scarlette followed suit, their curiosity piqued by the anticipation in the air. As they found a spot near the front of the stage, the music began to play, and the dancers leapt into action with grace and skill.

The rhythm of the music pulsed through the air, captivating the audience and drawing them into the energetic performance. The dancers moved with precision and passion, their movements fluid and mesmerizing.

Lyra clapped and cheered along with the crowd, her eyes shining with admiration. "They're incredible! I wish I could move like that."

Alex grinned, his gaze fixed on the performers with admiration. "They make it look so effortless! It's like they were born to dance."

Marcus nodded in agreement, his appreciation for the artistry evident on his face. "Indeed. It takes a lot of dedication and talent to perform like that."

Scarlette watched in awe, a sense of joy filling her heart. "It's moments like these that remind us of the beauty and creativity in the world. We should never take it for granted."

As the performance came to an end, the crowd erupted into applause, their cheers echoing throughout the park. The dancers took their final bows, their smiles bright with satisfaction.

The group joined in the applause, their spirits lifted by the uplifting performance. With smiles on their faces and warmth in their hearts, they continued their journey through the theme park, grateful for the memories they had created together.

After the exhilarating ride, they wandered through the theme park, sampling the various attractions and games on offer. From enchanted mazes to daring feats of acrobatics, there was no shortage of entertainment to be found in Esmeria.

But it was the peculiar red glowing fruits that caught their attention the most. Dubbed "Kung Fu Fruits" by the eccentric vendor Dippy, these otherworldly delicacies were said to grant temporary martial arts powers to those who consumed them.

"Sounds too good to be true," Marcus remarked sceptically, eyeig the fruits with suspicion.

As they strolled through the vibrant area of the otherworldly theme park, Marcus, Alex, Lyra, and Scarlette stumbled upon a captivating game called "Dragon's Hoop Toss." The booth was adorned with intricate dragon motifs, and the air buzzed with excitement as participants lined up to test their skills.

Alex's eyes lit up with determination as he surveyed the game, his competitive spirit urging him to give it a try. "This looks like fun! Who's up for a challenge?" he exclaimed, a grin spreading across his face as he glanced at his friends.

Lyra eagerly stepped forward, her eyes gleaming with anticipation. "Count me in! I've always been good at tossing things," she declared, her confidence shining through.

Marcus and Scarlette exchanged amused glances, knowing full well the playful rivalry that often ensued when their friends engaged in games of skill. But they were more than happy to join in the fun, eager to see who would emerge victorious. they approached the Dragon's Hoop Toss booth and eagerly handed over their tokens to the attendant, who greeted them with a friendly smile.

"Welcome, brave adventurers, to the Dragon's Hoop Toss challenge!" the attendant announced, gesturing towards the row of colourful hoops and the towering dragon-shaped targets beyond. "The rules are simple—toss the hoops onto the dragon's horns, and if you land one, you'll win a prize fit for a champion!"

Excitement bubbled within as they each took turns tossing the hoops, their competitive spirits driving them to do their best. Cheers and laughter filled the air as they celebrate, each successful throw earns them an assortment of prizes ranging from plush toys to enchanted trinkets.

But it was the grand prize a mysterious and oddly looking round red glowing fruit that caught their attention the most. Dippy, the eccentric vendor manning the booth, grinned mischievously as he presented it to them. "This, my friends, is no ordinary fruit," Dippy explained, his eyes twinkling with excitement. "It's called a 'Kung Fu Fruit,' and legend has it that once eaten, it grants the consumer temporary martial arts powers!"

The friends exchanged incredulous looks, unsure whether to believe Dippy's outlandish claims.

But the allure of such a mysterious and fantastical prize was too much to resist.

"Well, I've never been one to turn down a challenge," Alex declared, his eyes gleaming with determination as he stepped forward to take his turn at the Dragon's Hoop Toss.

With a flick of his wrist, Alex sent the hoop sailing through the air, his aim true as it landed squarely on the dragon's horn with a satisfying clang. The crowd erupted into cheers and applause, applauding Alex's impressive display of skill and accuracy.

As the attendant congratulated him on his victory, Alex's heart swelled with pride as he claimed the grand prize—the coveted Kung Fu Fruit. The friends erupted into laughter and cheers, their spirits buoyed by the thrill of victory and the promise of adventure that lay ahead.

As Marcus, Alex, Lyra, and Scarlette revelled in the festivities of 'The Battle of Dimensions' celebration, their laughter went through the air, mingling with the joyous sounds of the crowd.

The aroma of spices and herbs filled the air as Alex, Marcus, and Scarlette settled into a cozy corner of the Esmerian marketplace. Colorful tents with intricate designs lined the cobblestone streets, each one offering a tantalizing array of local delicacies.

"I can't believe we finally made it to Esmeria!" Scarlette exclaimed, her eyes sparkling with excitement as she perused the menu. "I've heard their food is out of this world."

Marcus nodded in agreement, his mouth already watering at the thought of indulging in Esmerian cuisine. "I've been dreaming about trying their famous dishes ever since we started planning this trip. I hope it lives up to the hype."

As their orders arrived, carried by a cheerful Esmerian server adorned in vibrant robes, the trio's attention turned to the tantalizing spread before them. Plates piled high with steaming delicacies were set before them, each dish more enticing than the last.

Alex's gaze lingered on a platter of golden-brown pastries filled with savory meat and fragrant spices. "Wow, these look amazing! What are they called?"

The server beamed with pride as he explained, "Those are our famous Esmerian meat pies, made with a secret blend of herbs and spices passed down through generations. They're a favorite among locals and travelers alike."

Scarlette's eyes lit up at the sight of a colorful salad adorned with ripe fruits and crisp vegetables. "And what's this?" she inquired, her curiosity piqued.

"That's our Esmerian summer salad, featuring the freshest ingredients from our local farms," the server replied, his voice filled with pride. "It's the perfect balance of sweet and savory, with a tangy dressing made from our signature Esmerian vinegar."

As they dug into their meal, the trio exchanged delighted exclamations with each bite. The meat pies were a symphony of flavors, with tender meat enveloped in flaky pastry and aromatic spices dancing on their tongues

Marcus took a sip of the strawberry brew, his eyes widening in delight at the burst of flavor that exploded on his palate. "This brew is incredible! It's like drinking sunshine in a glass."

The server chuckled at Marcus's enthusiasm, pleased to see his guests enjoying the fruits of Esmerian hospitality. "Ah, yes, our strawberry brew is a beloved Esmerian tradition. Made from the juiciest strawberries grown in our sun-kissed fields, it's the perfect way to cool off on a hot day."

As they savored their meal, Alex, Marcus, and Scarlette couldn't help but feel a sense of contentment wash over them.

But just as they were enjoying themselves in the excitement of the moment, a sudden shift in the atmosphere disrupted the festivities. The sky darkened ominously, and a cold chill swept through the air.

At first, they thought it was merely a passing storm, but the truth soon became apparent –A dark supernatural storm, unlike anything they had ever seen, descended upon Esmeria with terrifying force, leaving destruction in its wake.

"What's happening?" Alex shouted above the deafening roar of the storm, his voice barely audible over the howling winds.

Scarlette's eyes widened in alarm as she surveyed the destruction wrought by the dark storm. "I don't know, but we need to find shelter – and quickly," she replied, her voice tinged with urgency.

# CHAPTER SIX

## ZYRO'S ATTACK

Vesta, the guardian of Esmeria, was caught off guard before she could react, the storm descended upon Esmeria with ferocious intensity, unleashing its wrath upon the unsuspecting realm.

Vesta's guards, valiant though they were, stood no chance against the onslaught of dark storm creatures, shape-shifting shadows that moved with terrifying speed and agility.

Vesta herself was not spared from the storm's wrath. As bolts of dark energy lashed out, she fought with all her might to protect her people, her powers waning with each passing moment.

As the tempest raged on, a figure emerged from the darkness, its presence commanding and foreboding. Zyro, a name whispered in fear had returned with his legion of Dark Strom creatures. These beings, born of shadow and malice, prowled the land like phantoms, their forms shifting and contorting with a sinister grace.

Zyro, once a loyal warrior of Esmeria, is now consumed by envy and ambition. Zyro, his visage twisted by dark magic, appeared as a monstrous beast, clad in obsidian armour that gleamed with an otherworldly sheen.

As the chaos of the dark storm is ongoing, Vesta's powers

wane but her spirit is undiminished. It was then that Zyro, the dark sorcerer whose malevolent presence loomed over the realm like a shadow, made his presence known.

Zyro's dark form materialized before Vesta, his eyes gleaming with malice as he surveyed the destruction he had wrought. "Vesta," he sneered, his voice dripping with venom. "You thought you could stand against me, but you are no match for my power."

Vesta met Zyro's gaze with steely resolve, her voice steady despite the exhaustion that weighed heavily upon her. "Your reign of terror ends here, Zyro," she declared, her words echoing with authority. "I will not allow you to destroy everything we have worked so hard to protect."

Zyro laughed, a sound devoid of humour as he advanced towards Vesta with predatory grace. "You cannot stop me, Vesta," he taunted, his voice low and menacing. "You are weak, and your powers are fading. Soon, Esmeria will be mine, and there is nothing you can do to stop it."

But Vesta refused to back down, her determination unwavering in the face of Zyro's arrogance. "You underestimate the strength of our people," she countered, her voice ringing with defiance. "We will never surrender to you, no matter what darkness you unleash upon us."

Zyro's eyes flashed with fury at Vesta's defiance, his patience wearing thin as he realized that she would not yield to his demands. "You may be brave, Vesta," he growled, his voice laced with menace, "but your bravery will be your downfall.

Esmeria will fall, and you will watch helplessly as everything you hold dear is consumed by darkness."

The sudden destruction had weakened Vesta to the point of exhaustion, her very life force draining away with every passing second. With her forces scattered and overwhelmed, she knew that their only hope lay in retreating to the safety of the palace, where she could enact a last line of defence against Zyro,

Vesta, the revered ruler of Esmeria, stood amidst the chaos, her heart heavy with dread as she beheld the havoc wrought by Zyro's dark forces.

With grim determination, Vesta rallied her remaining forces, her loyal guards and warriors standing steadfastly by her side. Together, they fought valiantly against the tide of darkness, but it was a losing battle. Zyro's dark Storm creatures, grotesque manifestations of shadow and malice, seemed to multiply with each passing moment, their sinister forms twisting and contorting with unnatural grace as they laid waste to everything in their path.

As Vesta and her warriors made their way through the chaos, Vesta could feel the weight of her impending demise pressing down upon her like a suffocating shroud. The injuries she had sustained in the battle with Zyro had left her weak and vulnerable, her strength fading with each laboured breath.

Upon reaching the palace, Vesta wasted no time in summoning the last vestiges of her power to erect a protective shield around its walls. It was a desperate gambit, born of necessity and fueled by the dwindling embers of her strength. The shield shimmered with an ethereal glow, a barrier of light that stood as the last line of defence against Zyro's relentless advance.

But even as Vesta poured her remaining energy into maintaining the shield, she knew that her efforts might be in vain. For she was not only fighting against Zyro and his dark forces but also against the inexorable march of time itself. As the thunderous roar of Zyro's dark storm echoed through the air, Vesta knew that the fate of her kingdom hung in the balance. With every fibre of her being, she vowed to fight to her last breath, to defy the darkness and protect her people, no matter the cost. For she was Vesta, the guardian of Esmeria, and her resolve was unbreakable, even in the face of certain death.

As the remnants of Zyro's dark storm swirled ominously overhead, Dippy, the trusty companion of Alex, relayed crucial information about the secret weapon hidden within Vesta's palace. The gravity of the situation weighed heavily on the group as they huddled together in the dimly lit hideout, their faces etched with worry and uncertainty.

"Dippy, are you sure about this?" Alex questioned, his voice tinged with a hint of scepticism. "A secret weapon hidden in Vesta's palace sounds like something out of a fairy tale."

Dippy's mechanical whirr filled the air as he projected a hologram of the palace grounds, highlighting the location of the components which are *"the magical fuel, the crystal battery and the third one is self-roaming magical steering"* needed to repair for the fighter jet. "Absolutely, Alex," Dippy replied, his digital voice carrying an air of certainty. "The intelligence we've gathered indicates that Vesta has been developing a powerful weapon in secret, hidden deep within the halls of her palace. This weapon has the potential to turn the tide of the war in our favour, but acquiring it won't be easy."

Alex leaned forward, his brow furrowed in concentration. "What do we need to do?"

"We'll need to gather the components necessary to repair the fighter jet," Dippy explained, his holographic display shifting to reveal detailed schematics of the aircraft. "The jet is our only means of reaching Vesta's palace before he unleashes his full power. But the components are scattered throughout Esmeria, hidden in remote locations to prevent detection by Zyro's forces."

A sense of urgency crept into Dippy's voice as he continued, "Once we've collected all the components, we'll need to find an old scientist who specializes in aeronautics. He's the only one who can help us assemble the components and get the fighter jet operational again. Without him, our mission will be doomed to failure."

Alex nodded grimly, his mind already racing with plans and strategies. "Understood. We'll gather the components and find the scientist. But time is against us, and Zyro won't sit idly by while we make our preparations."

"Indeed," Dippy agreed. "Zyro's forces will be searching for the same components, and his dark storm grows stronger with each passing day. We must move swiftly if we're to have any hope of stopping him."

"Dippy, where did you learn about this fighter jet and the old scientist?" Alex asked, his curiosity piqued by the sudden revelation.

Dippy's mechanical whirr filled as he adjusted his holographic projections, his digital eyes flickering with data streams. "Alex, my knowledge stems from years of extensive data analysis and reconnaissance missions," Dippy began. "While you were busy leading the resistance against Zyro's forces, I was scouring every available database for information that could aid our cause."

The holographic display shifted, showing images of encrypted files and intercepted transmissions. "I stumbled upon classified documents detailing Vesta's research into advanced weaponry," Dippy continued. "Among them was information about a prototype fighter jet hidden within Esmeria — a relic from the days before Zyro's tyranny. It's been rumoured to possess capabilities far beyond those of conventional aircraft, which is why Vesta has kept it hidden away."

Alex nodded, understanding dawning on his face. "And the old scientist?"

Dippy nodded in response, his holographic display shifting once more to show images of an humanoid rabbit tinkering with machinery in a secluded workshop. "The scientist is a recluse who once worked for the royal family," Dippy explained. "He was a pioneer in the field of aeronautics, responsible for designing some of the kingdom's most advanced aircraft. But when Zyro seized power, the scientist went into hiding, fearing for his life."

"Finding him won't be easy," Alex remarked, his gaze lingering on the holographic image of the scientist. "But if he can help us repair the fighter jet, it might just be our ticket to victory."

Dippy nodded in agreement, his digital voice tinged with determination. "Indeed, Alex. With the fighter jet at our disposal, we'll have a chance to strike back against Zyro and his forces. But time is of the essence. We must act swiftly if we are to succeed."

The rest of the group listened intently as Dippy explained the origins of their mission, their resolve strengthened by the knowledge that they were not alone in their fight against the darkness that threatened to engulf their world.

As Dippy projected the hologram of the map, detailing their next steps in the mission, a sense of urgency filled the room. The holographic display shimmered with intricate details, showing the locations of the components needed to repair the fighter jet and the path to the wise scientist's hidden workshop.

But as the group leaned in to examine the map more closely, a sudden glitch rippled through Dippy's systems. His mechanical whirr stuttered, and his holographic projection flickered erratically. Before anyone could react, Dippy convulsed violently, his digital form fragmenting into pixels before their eyes.

"No, Dippy!" Alex cried out, reaching out futilely as his beloved companion disintegrated before him. Marcus and Scarlette watched in horror as Dippy's form dissolved into nothingness, leaving behind only a faint echo of his digital voice.

The room fell into stunned silence, the weight of Dippy's loss hanging heavy in the air. But their mourning was cut short by a sudden tremor that shook the hideout, causing the walls to groan and the ceiling to crack.

Outside, the once-pristine streets of Esmeria began to decay before their very eyes. Buildings crumbled, their facades crumbling like ancient ruins. Trees withered and died, their leaves turning to ash in the oppressive atmosphere of the dark storm.

"It's happening," Marcus whispered, his voice trembling with fear. "The dark storm is destroying everything."

With a sinking feeling in their hearts, they realized that they had no choice but to flee. The hideout offered little protection against the encroaching destruction and staying would only mean certain death.

Gathering what few belongings they could carry, Alex, Marcus, and Scarlette made their way through the crumbling streets of Esmeria, their footsteps echoing in the desolate silence. Behind them, the once-bustling city faded into oblivion, swallowed whole by the relentless onslaught of the dark storm.

As they escaped into the wilderness beyond the city limits, they cast one last glance back at the place they had once called home. But there was no time for nostalgia, no time to mourn what had been lost. For the dark storm raged on, its destructive power sparing nothing in its path.

As the dark storm's malevolent influence spread throughout Esmeria, a new horror emerged from its depths. Citizens who found themselves caught in the storm's sinister embrace were struck with a madness unlike anything the world had ever seen.

These unfortunate souls, their minds twisted and warped by the storm's corrupting influence, began to exhibit bizarre and grotesque behaviours. Some danced through the streets with wild abandon, their laughter echoing through the desolate alleys like the cackling of mad jesters. Others stumbled and staggered, their movements jerky and erratic, as if puppeteered by unseen hands. The most disturbing of all were those who succumbed to the madness completely, their once familiar faces contorted into grotesque caricatures of their former selves. With wide, manic eyes and twisted grins plastered across their faces, they wandered the streets in a daze, their laughter ringing hollow and discordant in the oppressive silence of the storm. amidst the chaos and madness, a new threat emerged. Shapeshifting shadow creatures, born from the very essence of the dark storm itself, prowled the streets with predatory intent. Their forms twisted and ever-shifting, they moved with a sinister grace, their red glowing eyes piercing the darkness like beacons of malevolence.

These creatures, drawn to the madness and despair that permeated the city, stalked their prey with relentless determination. And when they found their targets, they struck with deadly precision, their attacks leaving devastation in their wake.

The citizens of Esmeria, already driven to the brink of madness by the dark storm, were powerless to defend themselves against this new threat. Those who encountered the shadow creatures found themselves ensnared in a deadly game of cat and mouse, their every move watched and anticipated by their unseen assailants.

And yet, despite the danger that lurked around every corner, Alex, Marcus, and Scarlette pressed on, their determination unwavering in the face of overwhelming odds. They knew that the only way to survive was to keep moving, to avoid confrontation with the mad denizens of Esmeria and the shadow creatures that hunted them.

They moved further into the heart of the storm, their eyes scanning the shadows for any sign of danger. And though their path was fraught with peril, they refused to give in to despair, for they knew that the fate of Esmeria depended on their success.

They could feel the malevolent presence of the storm closing in around them, its icy tendrils reaching out to drag them. And though they fought with all their might to resist its grasp, they knew that their journey was far from over.

For the dark storm had unleashed horrors beyond imagining

upon the world,

As Alex, Marcus, and Scarlette tried to find a way through the treacherous streets of Esmeria, their hearts pounded with urgency. The looming threat of Zyro, now transformed into a colossal giant, sent shivers down their spines. His thunderous roars echoed ominously through the city, a constant reminder of the imminent danger they faced.

As they pressed forward, the trio encountered the remnants of Zyro's destructive rampage – overturned carts, shattered storefronts, and the occasional glimpse of terrified citizens fleeing for their lives.

With each thunderous roar that echoed through the streets, Alex felt the weight of their mission pressing down upon him. They had to reach Vesta's palace before Zyro found a way inside. The fate of Esmeria hung in the balance, and failure was not an option.

The streets were littered with obstacles – collapsed buildings, twisted wreckage, and the occasional skirmish between Zyro's minions and the few remaining defenders of Esmeria.

Despite the chaos that surrounded them, Alex and his friends pressed on, they knew that time was running out, and that every moment brought Zyro closer to achieving his sinister goals.

But they could not afford to falter, not when the fate of their kingdom hung in the balance. With grim determination, they forged ahead, their eyes fixed on the distant silhouette of Vesta's palace looming ominously on the horizon.

As they approached the palace grounds, the air crackled with tension, the very atmosphere thrumming with dark energy. And amidst the chaos, the distant sound of Zyro's thunderous roars served as a chilling reminder of the danger that lurked just beyond the palace walls.

As Alex, Marcus, and Scarlette's mission hung heavy in the air, each passing moment urged them forward in their quest to locate the scattered components.

# CHAPTER SEVEN

## THE SEARCH FOR THE COMPONENT

"We need to find those components as soon as possible," Alex murmured, his voice tinged with urgency. "Dippy said they're scattered throughout the city."

Marcus nodded in agreement, his lips curling into a confident smirk. "Agreed. The sooner we have everything we need, the sooner we can get out of here and make our way to the old scientist."

Scarlette's brow furrowed with concern as she glanced at the beleaguered citizens of Esmeria, their faces etched with weariness and despair. "But what about the people here?" she interjected, her voice soft yet resolute. "We can't just leave them to fend for themselves."

Alex paused, his gaze sweeping over the scene before them the shattered remnants of once-thriving homes, the weary faces of those who had lost everything, the distant rumble of Zyro's thunderous roars echoing through the city.

"We can't ignore the plight of our fellow citizens," Scarlette continued, her eyes blazing with determination. "They need our help now more than ever."

Marcus's smirk softened into a thoughtful frown as he considered Scarlette's words. "She's right," he conceded, his tone serious. "We can't turn a blind eye to the suffering around us. We must help however we can."

Alex nodded in agreement, a steely resolve settling over his features. "Then let's make a plan," he declared, his voice firm. "We'll split up and search for the components while also assisting anyone in need along the way. Every moment counts, but we won't abandon those who rely on us."

With their course of action decided, they encountered survivors in need of assistance – families searching for shelter, injured citizens in need of medical aid, and weary travellers seeking refuge from the storm.

"Please, you have to help us," a weary woman pleaded, her voice trembling with desperation. "We've been hiding here since the storm hit, but we're running out of supplies, and we don't know how much longer we can last."

Alex exchanged a worried glance with his companions before stepping forward with a reassuring smile. "We'll do everything we can to help," he assured them, his tone steady despite the turmoil raging around them. "Do you have any idea where we might find some provisions?"

The woman nodded, her eyes filled with gratitude. "There's a supply cache not too far from here," she explained, her voice barely above a whisper. "But it's in a dangerous part of the city, overrun with those... things."

Marcus clenched his fists, his jaw set with determination. "We'll take care of it," he declared, his voice unwavering. "You all stay here and keep hidden. We'll be back before you know it."

With a nod of agreement, Alex, Marcus, and Scarlette set off towards the supply cache, their senses on high alert for any sign of danger.

"These poor souls," Scarlette murmured, her voice heavy with sorrow, as they passed by a group of citizens engaged in a bizarre dance macabre, their movements jerky and disjointed. Alex's heart ached at the sight, but he knew they couldn't afford to dwell on the madness surrounding them. They had a mission to complete, and the lives of those depending on them hung in the balance.

Finally, they reached the supply cache, a nondescript building hidden away amidst the ruins of Esmeria. Marcus cautiously approached the door, his hand resting on the hilt of his weapon as he scanned the area for any signs of danger.

"All clear," he called out, his voice low but confident. With a nod of approval, Alex pushed open the door, revealing shelves stocked with much-needed provisions – food, water, medical supplies, and other essentials.

As they gathered what they could carry, a sudden noise from outside caught their attention – the telltale sound of shuffling footsteps and guttural growls.

"They've found us," Scarlette whispered, her eyes widening in alarm. Without hesitation, Alex and Marcus sprang into action, weapons at the ready as they prepared to defend themselves and the supplies they had gathered.

But as the shadowy figures emerged from the darkness, their forms shifting and twisting with malevolent intent, Alex knew that this would be their toughest battle yet.

With a fierce battle cry, Alex lunged forward, his sword slicing through the air with deadly precision as he met the first of the shadow creatures head-on. Marcus followed suit, his movements fluid and graceful as he dispatched another foe with a series of swift strikes.

Scarlette stood her ground, her D-blaster (A weapon also known as a "Dimension Blaster" that Blasts Interdimensional foes which they kept from their last adventure) ready as she aimed at the approaching enemies despite their skill and determination, the shadow creatures seemed endless in their numbers, their forms multiplying and shifting with each passing moment.

"We can't keep this up forever," Marcus grunted, his brow furrowed with concentration as he fended off another wave of attackers. "There's too many of them."

Alex gritted his teeth, his muscles burning with exertion as he fought to keep the creatures at bay. "We need to find another way out," he shouted over the din of battle. "We can't let them overwhelm us."

As if in response to his words, Scarlette's eyes widened with realization as she spotted a narrow alleyway leading away from the fray. "There," she called out, pointing towards the dimly lit passage. "We can make our escape through there."

With a nod of agreement, Alex and Marcus fought their way towards the alley, their weapons flashing in the darkness as they carved a path through the encroaching horde. Scarlette followed close behind, her arrows flying true as she provided cover fire for her companions.

Finally, they reached the relative safety of the alley, their chests heaving with exertion as they caught their breath. But their respite was short-lived, as the sound of approaching footsteps echoed ominously from the other end of the passage.

"We're not out of the woods yet," Marcus warned, his voice tense with anticipation. "We need to keep moving."

But despite the overwhelming odds stacked against them, Alex, Marcus, and Scarlette refused to give up hope. With each step they took, they drew closer to their goal – the scattered components needed to repair the fighter jet and turn the tide against the encroaching darkness.

For in the face of despair and destruction, they knew that their only choice was to keep moving forward, to fight for their survival and the survival of all those who called Esmeria home. And as they disappeared into the shadows of the city, their resolve burned brighter than ever, a beacon of hope in the darkest of times.

As Alex, Lyra, and the gang approached the abandoned theme park, they were met with a haunting sight. Once a vibrant and bustling attraction, the park now lay in ruin, its once-colourful attractions faded and overgrown with weeds. The entrance gate, once adorned with cheerful banners and flashing lights, now stood rusted and decrepit, its neon signs flickering feebly in the dim light.

"It's hard to believe this place used to be so lively," Alex remarked, his voice tinged with sadness as he surveyed the desolate scene before them.

Lyra nodded in agreement, her eyes scanning the dilapidated structures and overgrown pathways. "It's like a ghost town," she replied, her voice barely above a whisper. "I can't imagine what happened here."

As they entered the abandoned theme park, they encountered more signs of its former glory – remnants of once-thriving attractions now reduced to rubble, faded posters advertising long-forgotten shows and events, and empty food stalls now overrun by weeds and vines.

"It's like stepping into another world," Marcus mused, his voice filled with awe. "I never thought I'd see the day when this place would be abandoned."

Scarlette shuddered as she gazed around the surroundings. "It's giving me the creeps," she admitted, her voice trembling slightly. "I can't shake the feeling that we're being watched."

As they continued their search at the abandoned theme park, they encountered more unsettling sights – broken-down rides with missing pieces and twisted metal, faded murals depicting scenes of joy and laughter now obscured by layers of dust and decay.

"It's like a nightmare come to life," Lyra whispered, her voice barely audible over the creaking of the old rides and the rustling of the wind through the trees.

Alex nodded solemnly, his eyes scanning their surroundings for any sign of danger. "We need to stay focused," he declared, his voice firm. "We came here for a reason, and we won't let anything stop us from finding what we need."

"We need to find that component and get out of here as quickly as possible," Alex whispered, his voice tense with apprehension. "But we need to stay alert. The dark storm's influence has twisted this place into something... dangerous."

Lyra nodded in agreement, her eyes scanning their surroundings warily. "Agreed. Let's split up and search the area. We'll cover more ground that way, but be careful. The creatures spawned by the dark storm could be lurking anywhere."

As they started the search in the abandoned theme park, they encountered signs of the dark storm's influence – twisted, otherworldly creatures with glowing red eyes prowling the shadows, and possessed citizens driven to madness by its corrupting power.

Suddenly, a group of possessed citizens emerged from the shadows, their eyes vacant and their movements jerky and erratic. "They're coming!" Lyra shouted, her voice filled with urgency.

With no time to lose, Alex and Lyra led the gang on a frantic chase through the abandoned park, dodging the possessed citizens and the dark storm creatures at every turn. They raced through dilapidated attractions and overgrown pathways, their hearts pounding with adrenaline as they fought to stay one step ahead of their pursuers.

As they reached the heart of the park, they stumbled upon an old, decrepit roller coaster – its tracks twisted and warped, its cars rusted and creaking with age. "We can use this to escape!" Alex exclaimed, his voice barely audible over the roar of the dark storm.

With no other options left, they scrambled into the roller coaster cars and braced themselves as the ride lurched into motion. The ancient machinery groaned and protested as it climbed higher and higher, carrying them away from the clutches of their pursuers.

But their escape was short-lived. As they hurtled through the twisted loops and turns of the roller coaster, they were pursued by the dark storm creatures, their red eyes glowing with malice as they closed in on their prey.

With every twist and turn, Alex and Lyra fought to keep the gang safe, using every ounce of their strength and skill to outmanoeuvre their relentless pursuers. But as the ride reached its climax, they faced their most daunting challenge yet – a showdown with the dark storm creatures on the highest peak of the roller coaster.

With their backs against the wall, Alex, Lyra, and the gang rallied together, unleashing a flurry of attacks against their foes. Against all odds, they emerged victorious, the dark storm creatures vanquished and found the magic fuel for the fighter jet in the abandoned roller coaster cart ahead!

After their harrowing escape from the abandoned theme park, Alex, Marcus, and Scarlette embarked on the next leg of their journey to the forbidden tombs of Esmeria. Guided by the cryptic clues provided by Dippy before his untimely demise.

"Alright, team. The next component for the fighter jet is said to be in the forbidden tombs of Esmeria," Alex muttered, his voice low and determined.

"Forbidden tombs? Sounds ominous," Marcus echoed, his brow furrowing with concern.

"How do we even get there?" Scarlette added, her voice tinged with apprehension.

Alex paused, considering their options. "According to Dippy's last transmission, the tombs are located deep within the ancient forest on the outskirts of the city," he explained. "We'll have to navigate through the forest and find the entrance to the tombs."

Marcus nodded in understanding. "Got it. But what about the dangers that might await us in the forest?" he asked, his eyes scanning their surroundings warily.

"We'll need to stay alert and watch each other's backs," Alex replied, his tone resolute. "We've faced plenty of challenges before, and this will be no different. As long as we stick together, we can handle whatever comes our way."

As they journey into the forest, the air grows thick with the scent of earth and moss, and the sound of rustling leaves and distant wildlife fills their ears. But despite the tranquil surroundings, they remained vigilant, knowing that danger could lurk around any corner.

After what felt like hours of trekking through the dense

undergrowth, they finally stumbled upon the entrance to the forbidden tombs – a towering stone archway adorned with faded symbols and ancient runes.

"This must be it," Scarlette breathed, her eyes wide with awe.

"Let's not waste any time," Alex urged, his voice firm. "The longer we wait, the greater the chance that Zyro will beat us to the component. We need to find it and get out of here as quickly as possible."

With their hearts pounding in their chests, Alex, Marcus, and Scarlette descended into the forbidden tombs of Esmeria, a sense of foreboding. The ancient catacombs were shrouded in darkness, their walls lined with crypts and sarcophagi that seemed to whisper of long-forgotten secrets.

"We need to find that component quickly," Alex murmured, his voice echoing softly in the dimly lit chamber. "But we need to stay alert. Who knows what dangers lurk in these depths."

Marcus nodded in agreement; his expression determined. "Agreed. The sooner we have everything we need, the sooner we can get out of here and make our way to the scientist."

Scarlette's brow furrowed with concern as she glanced around at the ominous surroundings. "But what about the creatures that dwell in these tombs?" she interjected, her voice filled with apprehension. "We can't just leave them unchallenged. They could pose a threat to others if we don't stop them."

Alex paused, considering Scarlette's words carefully. "You're right," he conceded, his tone serious. "We can't afford to ignore the dangers that lurk in these tombs.

"We must tread carefully," Alex warned, his voice barely above a whisper. "These tombs are said to be guarded by powerful creatures and dark magic."

Marcus nodded, his gaze fixed on the shadowy entrance to the tombs. "Agreed. But we can't let fear hold us back. We need to find that component for the fighter jet and put an end to Zyro's reign of terror."

Scarlette's eyes darted nervously between her companions and the looming entrance to the tombs.

The walls were lined with ancient hieroglyphs and faded murals depicting scenes of death and decay, and the air was heavy with the scent of dust and decay.

"We must proceed with caution," Marcus urged, his voice hushed. "Who knows what ancient secrets lie hidden within these walls?"

Scarlette nodded in agreement, her eyes darting nervously around the dimly lit chamber. "Agreed," she replied, her voice barely above a whisper. "But we mustn't lose sight of our goal. The component for the fighter jet could be anywhere in these tombs, and we can't afford to waste any time."

With their hearts pounding in their chests, Alex, Marcus, and Scarlette pressed on into the depths of the tombs, their senses alert for any sign of danger.

As they moved, they encountered the undead creatures that lurked within – twisted, skeletal figures with hollow eyes and grasping claws. Their skeletal forms were twisted and contorted, with bones protruding at odd angles and jagged edges. Hollow eye sockets gleamed with malevolent energy, glowing with an otherworldly light that cast eerie shadows across their decaying features.

Their flesh, what remained of it, clung to their bones in tattered shreds, mottled with patches of rot and decay. Long, gnarled claws extended from their skeletal hands, their razor-sharp tips glinting ominously in the dim light of the tomb.

As they shuffled forward, their movements were jerky and disjointed, as if they were puppets being manipulated by unseen strings. A foul stench emanated from their decaying forms, filling the air with the sickly sweet scent of death and decay.

Despite their grotesque appearance, there was a sinister intelligence gleaming in their empty eye sockets, a malevolent awareness that spoke of dark and twisted desires.

As they advanced, their unearthly moans echoed through the tomb, sending shivers down the spines of all who heard them. It was clear that these creatures were not mere mindless zombies, but something far more sinister – a twisted mockery of life, animated by dark and malevolent forces beyond comprehension.

Alex tightened his grip on his weapon, a bead of sweat trickling down his brow as he braced himself.

With a bloodcurdling screech, the creatures launched themselves forward, their razor-sharp claws slashing through the air with deadly precision. Alex, Marcus, and Scarlette fought back with all their might, but it was clear that they were outnumbered and outmatched.

The air was thick with the sounds of battle – the clash of steel on bone, the desperate cries of the living, and the unearthly moans of the undead. Scarlette stumbled backward, a gash opening on her arm as she narrowly avoided a swipe from one of the creatures.

Marcus fared no better, his breath coming in ragged gasps as he fended off blow after blow. Despite their best efforts, the D-blasters didn't work against them.

The creatures seemed relentless, their numbers only growing as more emerged from the darkness.

Fear gnawed at Alex's insides as he fought tooth and nail to protect his friends, the weight of their impending doom pressing down on him like a suffocating blanket. It seemed as though there was no end to the horde, no escape from their relentless onslaught. The undead creatures keeps coming in multiples.

Just when it seemed that all hope was lost, Alex's hand closed around something small and familiar in his bag – the kung fu fruits they had acquired earlier. With a surge of determination, he withdrew them, the realization dawning on him that they might just be their last hope.

"Take these!" he shouted, tossing the fruits to Marcus and Scarlette as they fought for their lives. "They might just give us the edge we need to turn the tide!"

With renewed vigor, the trio bit into the fruits, their senses sharpening as a surge of energy coursed through their veins.

With newfound strength and resolve, they fought back against the undead horde with a ferocity born of desperation, each blow striking true and sending the creatures reeling.

Slowly but surely, they began to gain the upper hand, driving the creatures back with each passing moment. The tide of battle had turned, and victory seemed within their grasp as they fought tooth and nail to overcome their monstrous foes.

But even as they fought, a lingering sense of unease lingered in the air, a reminder that in the depths of the tombs, darkness lurked around every corner, waiting to claim them as its own.

As they bit into the fruits, they felt a surge of energy course through their bodies, their muscles tingling with strength and agility. With their new martial arts powers, they fought back against the undead creatures with renewed ferocity, striking them with powerful blows that sent them reeling back in shock.

With each punch and kick, the creatures were knocked back with a forceful shock blast, their undead forms crumbling beneath the onslaught of Alex and the gang's superhuman abilities. After the battle had ceased and the creatures were down they had spotted the crystal battery glistening in one of the empty coffins ahead.

As Alex, Marcus, and Scarlette emerged from the depths of the forbidden tombs, the encounter with the undead creatures had been harrowing, but they had emerged victorious, the component for the fighter jet in hand.

"We did it," Alex breathed, his voice tinged with disbelief as he examined the precious component they had retrieved. "We found it."

Marcus grinned, a sense of triumph evident in his expression. "Agreed. The sooner we have everything we need, the sooner we can get out of here and make our way to the scientist."

But Scarlette's brow furrowed with concern as she cast a glance back at the entrance to the tomb. "What about the others who may still be trapped down there?" she interjected; her voice filled with compassion. "We can't just leave them behind."

Alex nodded in agreement, his eyes scanning the darkened entrance to the tomb. "You're right," he conceded, his tone sombre. "We can't abandon anyone to the mercy of those creatures. We'll have to find a way to help them."

As they progressed in their search for the component in Esmeria, Alex, Marcus, and Scarlette encountered a frantic citizen searching for his lost pet despite their warnings to stay indoors and avoid the dark storm creatures. The man, a stout figure with wild eyes and dishevelled hair, seemed determined to carry on with his search, heedless of the dangers that lurked in the shadows.

"Sir, you really should reconsider," Alex urged, his voice laced with concern. "The storm creatures are out in full force tonight. It's not safe to be wandering around out here alone."

The man waved off Alex's warnings with a dismissive gesture, a stubborn glint in his eyes. "Nonsensc! My Fluffy wouldn't wander far. I'll have him back in no time," he declared, his voice filled with misplaced confidence.

Marcus stepped forward, his expression grave. "You don't understand. These creatures are not to be trifled with. They're ruthless and deadly. You need to get to safety before it's too late."

But the man simply scoffed, a derisive snort escaping his lips.

"I've lived in Esmeria my whole life. I know how to take care of myself," he retorted, his tone dripping with arrogance.

Scarlette stepped forward, her voice tinged with urgency. "Please, sir, listen to reason. We've seen what these creatures are capable of. They won't hesitate to attack if they sense you're vulnerable."

But despite their best efforts to persuade him otherwise, the man remained obstinate, determined to continue his search regardless of the risks.

With a resigned sigh, Alex exchanged a worried glance with his friends, knowing that they couldn't force the man to see reason.

"We can't just leave him out here," Scarlette insisted, her voice tinged with concern as they watched the man.

"He'll be easy prey for those creatures if we don't do something."

But before they could intervene further, they heard the anguished screams of the man as he was overcome by the dark storm creatures, his fate sealed by his foolishness. The sound sent a chill down their spines, a grim reminder of the unforgiving dangers that lurked in the shadows of Esmeria. With heavy hearts, Alex, Marcus, and Scarlette turned away, knowing that there was nothing more they could do for him now.

they stumbled upon a secluded cave nestled amidst the rocky terrain. Drawn by the sound of commotion and cries of terror emanating from within, they cautiously approached their senses on high alert.

Peering into the dimly lit cave, they were met with the sight of a peculiar figure huddled in the shadows –He was unlike anyone they had ever encountered before, with an otherworldly aura and a demeanour that seemed to exude annoyance and sarcasm in equal measure, a figure unlike any they had encountered before – a humanoid rabbit known as "Jix". the scientist.

With his keen, intelligent eyes shining in the low light, Jix exuded an aura of otherworldly intelligence that both fascinated and unnerved those who beheld him. His fur, a soft shade of silver-grey, seemed to shimmer in the faint glow of the cave, giving him an ethereal appearance that defied explanation.

As they cautiously approached, Jix regarded them with a mixture of curiosity and irritation, his whiskers twitching in annoyance as if he already knew their purpose for intruding upon his solitude. His demeanour, though refined and composed, hinted at a sharp wit and a penchant for sarcasm that matched his exceptional intellect

"Who goes there?" Jix's voice echoed through the cavern, his tone sharp and irritable as he regarded the newcomers with suspicion.

"We mean you no harm," Alex spoke up, his voice steady as he stepped forward into the cave. "We heard the screams and came to investigate. Are you alright?"

Jix snorted derisively, his eyes narrowing as he regarded them with scepticism. "Do I look alright to you?" he retorted, his tone dripping with sarcasm. "I've been hiding out here from those blasted Dark Storm creatures if you must know."

Scarlette's brow furrowed with concern as she took in the scientist's frazzled appearance. "We're sorry to hear that," she said sympathetically. "But we need your help. We're on a mission to stop Zyro and save Esmeria, and we need you to fire up the jet with the components we've collected."

Jix's eyes widened in surprise at the mention of Zyro's name, a flicker of fear crossing his features before he quickly masked it with a scowl. "And why should I help you?" he demanded, his tone defiant.

"Because if we don't stop Zyro, Esmeria will be lost," Marcus interjected his voice firm with determination. "We need all the help we can get, and you're our best chance at success."

Jix hesitated for a moment, weighing his options as he studied the determined expressions of Alex, Marcus, and Scarlette. Finally, with a resigned sigh, he relented. "Fine," he grumbled. "But don't expect me to do it out of the goodness of my heart. There's something in it for me, right?"

Alex nodded, a small smile playing at the corners of his lips. "Of course," he replied. "We'll make sure you're rewarded for your assistance. Now, can you tell us where we can find the last component we need?"

Jix's expression softened slightly as he regarded them with reluctant respect. "The last component is located in the lakes of Esmeria," he revealed, his tone serious. "But be warned – it won't be easy to retrieve. The lakes are guarded by powerful creatures and treacherous traps. You'll need all the help you can get if you want to succeed."

As Alex, Marcus, and Scarlette leave Jix's cave, With the scientist's reluctant agreement to help them and the knowledge of the last component's location, they set out towards the lakes of Esmeria, guided by Jix's directions.

"We need to make our way to the lakes," Alex said, his voice firm with determination as they trudged through the rugged terrain. "That's where we'll find the final component."

Marcus nodded, his eyes scanning the horizon for any signs of danger. "But how do we know where exactly in the lakes it's located?" he asked, furrowing his brow in thought.

Scarlette looked thoughtful for a moment before speaking up. "Jix mentioned something about an underwater city of Atlantis," she recalled, her voice tinged with uncertainty. "Perhaps that's where we'll find the component."

As they continued on their journey, their surroundings grew increasingly unfamiliar, the landscape giving way to dense forests and rocky cliffs. But despite the obstacles that lay before them, just as they began to worry that they had lost their way, they stumbled upon a narrow path that led towards the shimmering waters of the lakes.

"We're getting close," Alex said, his voice filled with excitement as they approached the edge of the lake. "Now we just need to find a way to reach Atlantis."

As they stood at the water's edge, the tranquil surface of the lake stretched out before them, reflecting the clear blue sky above like a flawless mirror. Tall, majestic trees framed the scene, their verdant branches swaying gently in the breeze, creating a soothing melody of rustling leaves.

Marcus squinted against the sunlight, gazing over the shimmering expanse of water. "It's hard to believe that such beauty hides such danger," he remarked, his voice tinged with a mixture of awe and apprehension.

Scarlette nodded in agreement, her eyes scanning the horizon for any signs of movement. "The calm surface of the lake can be deceiving," she added, her tone serious. "But we can't let our guard down, not with what's at stake."

Alex tightened the straps of his wetsuit, his expression determined. "Agreed. We need to stay focused and keep our wits about us," he declared, his voice firm with resolve. "The component we're searching for could be the key to defeating Zyro once and for all."

They waded into the cool, refreshing waters, the gentle lapping of the waves soothing their nerves as they prepared for the dive ahead. Marcus led the way, his movements fluid and confident as he submerged himself beneath the surface with a powerful stroke of his arms.

As Alex and Scarlette followed suit, the outside world faded away, replaced by the tranquil embrace of the underwater realm. Sunlight filtered down through the crystal-clear water, illuminating the ancient ruins of Atlantis that lay hidden below.

Scarlette marvelled at the sight, her eyes wide with wonder as she took in the majestic architecture of the submerged city. "It's like something out of a fairy tale," she breathed, her voice hushed with awe.

Alex nodded in agreement, his focus fixed on the task at hand. "Let's stay on track," he reminded them, his tone steady and determined. "We need to find that component before the sea creature finds us."

As they swam deeper into Atlantis, their eyes scanned the underwater landscape for any sign of their elusive quarry. And then, just as it seemed they would never find it, they spotted a glimmering object nestled amidst the ruins "A golden power boosting joy stick"-the final piece of the puzzle they had been searching for.

With a triumphant cry, they swam towards it, their movements swift and sure as they closed in on their prize. But their moment of victory was short-lived, as a massive shadow loomed overhead, casting a dark pall over the underwater landscape.

"We need to get out of here," Marcus urged, his voice tinged with urgency as they watched the creature's approach. "Now!" their hearts pounding in their chests as they swam for their lives. The leviathan's massive jaws snapped at their heels, its powerful tail thrashing through the water as it pursued them with relentless determination.

But just as it seemed they would be swallowed whole by the monstrous creature; they spotted a glimmer of light in the distance – the fabled underwater city of Atlantis. With renewed determination, they swam towards it, their lungs burning with exertion as they drew closer and closer.

As the colossal sea creature loomed closer, its monstrous form casting a shadow over Alex, Marcus, and Scarlette, panic threatened to consume them.

"We need to swim towards that light," Alex shouted over the crashing waves, his voice filled with urgency as they struggled to keep ahead of the creature's relentless pursuit. "It might be our only chance to escape!" After a close encounter with the leviathan swimming towards them and opening its jaw with jagged teeth ready to devour them, they managed to swim toward the light and an exhilarating sensation came over them.

As they emerged on the other side, they found themselves in a bright and colourful bonus stage, the air filled with the scent of sweet Esmerian treats and the sound of joyous laughter. Before them lay a table laden with an array of delicious delicacies – candies, pastries, and fruits of every shape and colour.

"Look at all this," Marcus exclaimed, his eyes wide with

wonder as he surveyed the bounty before them. "It's like a dream come true!"

Scarlette grinned, her spirits lifted by the sight of the treats. "I don't know about you, but I could use a pick-me-up after that ordeal," she said, reaching eagerly for a piece of candy.

As they indulged in the special Esmerian treats, they felt a surge of energy coursing through their bodies, invigorating them and revitalizing their weary spirits. But amidst the revelry, Alex's eyes fell upon something shimmering amidst the pile of treats – a gleaming gold coin, pulsing with an otherworldly power.

"What's this?" he murmured, reaching out to pick up the coin. As his fingers closed around it, he felt a surge of power coursing through him, filling him with a sense of strength and resilience, unlike anything he had ever experienced before.

"It's the Gold 'Power' Ghost Coin," Marcus exclaimed, his eyes widening in awe as he recognized the significance of the artefact. "With that, you'll have the strength of ten men!"

But their moment of discovery was interrupted by a strange sensation – the ground beneath their feet began to tremble, and the air grew thick with tension. Before they could react, a voice echoed through the chamber, filled with both menace and intrigue.

"Ah, so you've found my little bonus stage," the voice said, its tone dripping with sarcasm and amusement. "How quaint."

As they turned to face the source of the voice, they were met with the sight of a mysterious figure standing before them – a cloaked figure with glowing eyes and a mischievous grin.

# CHAPTER EIGHT

## THE PUZZLE IN THE PALACE

"I am the Keeper of the Bonus Stage," the figure proclaimed, gesturing towards the table of treats with a flourish. "And you, my friends, have stumbled upon my domain. But fear not – you are welcome to partake in my offerings if you dare."

With a sense of curiosity and caution, Alex, Marcus, and Scarlette exchanged wary glances before cautiously approaching the cloaked figure.

As the gang emerged from the bright and colourful bonus stage, their hands clutching the newly acquired ICE Blasters, they found themselves back in the dense forests of Esmeria. The air crackled with tension as they prepared for the inevitable battle ahead.

Alex's grip tightened around the handle of his ICE Blaster, his jaw set in determination. "We need to be ready for anything," he said, his voice steady despite the adrenaline coursing through his veins. "The Dark Storm Creatures won't go down without a fight."

Lyra nodded in agreement, her eyes scanning the surrounding forest for any sign of movement. "We can't afford to let our guard down," she cautioned, her voice low with urgency. "They could be lurking anywhere, waiting to strike."

The scientist, Jix, eyed the ICE Blasters warily, his expression a mix of curiosity and apprehension. "These weapons may be powerful, but they won't be enough to take down every creature in Zyro's army," he warned, his voice tinged with doubt. "We need to choose our battles wisely."

But before they could formulate a plan, the forest erupted into chaos as the Dark Storm Creatures descended upon them with ferocious speed. Alex raised his ICE Blaster, unleashing a barrage of freezing blasts that struck their targets with deadly accuracy.

The creatures shrieked in agony as they were encased in ice, their forms shattering into a thousand frozen fragments upon impact. Yet for every creature they defeated, two more seemed to take its place, their numbers seemingly endless.

Marcus and Scarlette fought alongside them, their ICE Blasters blazing as they held the creatures at bay. But their victory was short-lived, as a deafening crack echoed through the forest, followed by the sickening sound of splintering wood.

A massive tree crashed to the ground, its branches tearing through the air like deadly projectiles. Marcus and Scarlette were caught in the path of destruction, their bodies struck down by the falling debris.

"NO!" Alex cried out in horror, his heart-shattering at the sight of his fallen comrades. Lyra's eyes widened in disbelief, her hands shaking with grief as she knelt beside their lifeless forms.

Jix's normally stoic demeanour faltered, his features contorted with sorrow as he surveyed the devastation around them. "We can't stay here," he said, his voice heavy with emotion. "There are still too many of them. We need to retreat."

With a heavy heart, Alex nodded in agreement, his eyes burning with unshed tears as he turned away from the fallen bodies of his friends. "Let's go," he said, his voice barely above a whisper. "We'll honour their memory by finishing what we started."

And so, with a heavy heart Alex, Lyra, and Jix turned and fled into the depths of the forest, leaving behind the fallen heroes who had sacrificed everything in the fight against darkness.

As they fled into the forest, the weight of loss hung heavy upon them, each step a painful reminder of the sacrifices made

"We can't let their deaths be in vain," Alex declared, his voice a quiet yet resolute whisper. "We have to keep moving forward, no matter what."

Lyra nodded, her eyes shining with determination despite the tears that streaked her cheeks. "They believed in us," she said softly, her voice catching with emotion. "We have to believe in ourselves too."

Jix's expression was grim as he led the way, his senses sharp for any sign of danger. "We must find a way to honour their memory," he said, his voice tinged with regret. "But for now, our priority is survival."

the echoes of battle still ringing in their ears, they encountered more of the Dark Storm Creatures lurking in the shadows.

With grim determination, they unleashed the power of their ICE Blasters, freezing their enemies in their tracks before pressing on.

But with each passing moment, the weight of their loss threatened to overwhelm them. Marcus and Scarlette had been more than just comrades-in-arms; they had been friends, confidants, and pillars of strength in the darkest of times.

In the realms of the living and the dead, Marcus and Scarlette found themselves suddenly back in the familiar streets of London. Their forms materialized amidst the city, invisible to all but themselves and any who possessed the gift of second sight.

Marcus blinked in disbelief, his translucent figure shimmering in the soft glow of the streetlights. "Are we... back in London?" he questioned, his voice carrying a mixture of astonishment.

Scarlette nodded, "It seems so," she confirmed, her voice tinged with a ghostly echo. "But how? And why?"

As they pondered their unexpected return to the mortal realm, a gentle breeze swept through the air, carrying with it the distant murmur of voices and the faint scent of city life. It was as if the very fabric of London itself was welcoming them home.

"We need to figure out what brought us back here," Marcus declared, his eyes scanning the familiar streets with curiosity. "There must be a reason for it."

Scarlette nodded in agreement, her gaze drifting toward a nearby figure moving through the crowd. "Look," she whispered, pointing toward a familiar face that seemed to shimmer with an otherworldly light. "Isn't that... Lucas?"

Marcus followed her gaze, his ghostly features contorted in a mixture of surprise and concern. "It is," he confirmed, his voice low with uncertainty.

"Scarlette, let's pay Lucas and his friends a visit," Marcus whispered, his voice carrying a spectral echo.

Scarlette nodded, her translucent form shimmering in the moonlight. "Agreed, Marcus. It's time they faced the consequences of their actions."

they made their way to the abandoned warehouse where Lucas and his gang often congregated. As they phased through the walls, they were met with the sight of Lucas and his friends gathered around a flickering candle, their faces contorted in shadows.

Marcus and Scarlette exchanged a knowing glance before slipping into the shadows, ready to unleash their ghostly presence upon the unsuspecting group.

With a subtle flicker of their ghostly fingers, Marcus and Scarlette began to possess objects within the warehouse, causing them to tremble and shake as if possessed by unseen forces. The air grew thick with an otherworldly chill as whispers filled the air, sending shivers down the spines of Lucas and his gang.

"What's going on?" Lucas exclaimed, his voice trembling with fear as he glanced around the room.

But Marcus and Scarlette remained unseen, their ghostly forms hidden from view as they continued to torment their unwitting victims. They caused objects to levitate and furniture to move of its own accord, all the while emitting moans and groans that echoed through the warehouse like the wails of tormented souls.

Lucas and his gang huddled together in terror, their bravado crumbling in the face. It soon became clear to them that they were no match for the vengeful spirits that haunted the warehouse, and with each passing moment, their fear grew more palpable.

The flickering candle cast grotesque shadows upon the walls, twisting and contorting as if alive with malevolent intent. Suddenly, the flames sputtered and died, plunging the room into darkness.

"Please, make it stop!" Lucas pleaded, his voice quivering with desperation.

But Marcus and Scarlette showed no mercy, their ghostly laughter echoing through the darkness as they continued to unleash their spectral wrath upon the terrified group. It was a haunting unlike any they had ever experienced, a chilling reminder of the consequences of their malevolent deeds.

We have to do something," one of Lucas's friends muttered, his voice trembling with fear. "We can't just keep running."

Lucas nodded, his mind racing with thoughts of the horrors they had witnessed back in the warehouse. "But what can we do?" he asked, his voice barely above a whisper. "We're no match for ghosts."

Another member of the group spoke up, his voice tinged with desperation. "Maybe we can make amends somehow," he suggested. "Maybe if we apologize for what we've done, they'll leave us alone."

Lucas considered the idea for a moment, weighing the possibility of redemption against the overwhelming fear that still gripped him. "It's worth a try," he finally conceded.

With a deep breath, Lucas stepped forward, his voice trembling as he spoke into the darkness. "We're sorry," he called out, his words echoing through the empty space. "We're sorry for everything we've done."

For a moment, there was only silence, the stillness of the night broken only by the sound of their ragged breathing. And then, from the depths of the darkness, came a soft whisper, barely audible but filled with a sense of forgiveness.

"Thank you," the voice murmured, its tone gentle yet tinged with sadness. "Thank you for acknowledging your mistakes."

Lucas and his gang exchanged uncertain glances, their hearts heavy with the weight of their guilt. But as they stood there in the darkness, a sense of peace washed over them, a glimmer of hope amidst the shadows.

And as they turned to leave the warehouse behind, they knew that they had been given a second chance—a chance to make amends for the wrongs they had committed and to walk a path of redemption.

That fateful night, as the city shrouded in darkness, Marcus and Scarlette stumbled upon a clandestine meeting between the Mayor and "Mr. Big" and her ex boyfriend Samuel in the shadows of an abandoned alleyway. Hidden from view, they listened intently as the two conspirators plotted their next move, their voices thick with malice and greed.

"We must silence anyone who threatens to expose our operation," the Mayor hissed, his eyes glinting with malevolence. "Yes we cannot afford to let our secrets be revealed." Samuel coldly added.

"Agreed," "Mr. Big" replied, his voice dripping with contempt. "But we must also ensure that 'The Hood' continues to sow chaos and fear throughout the city. It is our greatest weapon against those who would oppose us."

Marcus and Scarlette exchanged a silent glance, their resolve was not to allow the Mayor, "Mr. Big" and Samuel to continue their reign of terror unchecked. It was time to bring their dark deeds into the light and expose them for the villains they truly were.

With a flicker of his ghostly fingers, Marcus summoned a spectral gust of wind, causing a nearby stack of crates to topple over with a resounding crash. The Mayor, "Mr. Big" and Samuel whirled around in alarm, their faces contorted in shock as they realized they were no longer alone.

"Who's there?" the Mayor demanded, his voice trembling with fear.

"We are the spirits of justice," Scarlette replied, her voice carrying a ghostly echo. "And we have come to expose your crimes."

With a sense of grim satisfaction, Marcus and Scarlette revealed themselves to the Mayor, "Mr. Big," and Samuel their translucent forms shimmering in the darkness like apparitions from another world. The Mayor and Samuel's eyes widened in horror as he realized the truth of their words, while "Mr. Big" sneered in defiance, his lips curled into a cruel smirk.

"You cannot stop us," the Mayor spat, his voice filled with arrogance. "We are untouchable."

With a flicker of their ghostly fingers, they summoned a spectral storm of swirling mist and shadow, enveloping the Mayor and "Mr. Big" in an otherworldly embrace.

As the darkness closed in around them, the Mayor, "Mr. Big" and Samuel were overcome with a sense of dread unlike anything they had ever known. They thrashed and struggled against the spectral bonds that held them captive, their cries of defiance drowned out by the echoing laughter of the spirits that surrounded them.

And then, with a blinding flash of light, the darkness was dispelled, revealing the Mayor, "Mr. Big" and Samuel bound in chains of ethereal energy, their faces pale with terror as they stared into the empty void of the night.

"You have been judged and found wanting," Marcus declared, his voice echoing with the authority of the grave. "Your reign of terror ends here."

With his ghostly hand, Marcus summoned the authorities.

As the authorities arrived on the scene, Marcus and Scarlette watched from the shadows, their ghostly forms obscured by the veil of night. With a sense of grim satisfaction, they witnessed the Mayor, "Mr. Big" and Samuel being led away in handcuffs, their faces pale with fear as they realized the gravity of their crimes.

"You cannot do this to us!" the Mayor protested, his voice filled with desperation.

But the officers paid no heed to his pleas, their expressions stern as they escorted the two men into waiting police cars. As the vehicles pulled away into the night, Marcus and Scarlette exchanged a silent nod, their mission finally complete.

But their victory was short-lived, for even as they faded into the darkness, a sense of unease lingered in the air. They knew that the Mayor and "Mr. Big" would not go down without a fight, and that the battle for justice was far from over.

In the dead of night, as the moon cast its silvery glow over the quiet suburban streets of Alex's hometown, a sinister presence lurking in the shadows. The Dark Storm creatures, sent by the malevolent Zyro, slithered and skulked around the perimeter of Alex's family home,

Inside the cosy confines of the house, Alex's mother, Joanna Knight, and her husband, Paul, sat in the living room, their faces etched with worry as they watched the evening news.

"It's been days since we heard from Alex," Joanna murmured, her voice tinged with anxiety as she clutched the remote control in her trembling hands. "I can't shake this feeling that something's wrong."

Paul nodded in silent agreement, his brow furrowed with concern as he glanced out the window, where shadows seemed to dance in the moonlight. "I know, dear," he replied, his voice heavy with worry. "I just wish there was something we could do to help him."

As if in response to their shared fears, a sudden noise erupted outside, shattering the quiet of the night. The Dark Storm creatures, sensing their prey within reach, unleashed a barrage of unearthly howls and shrieks, sending a shiver down the spines of Joanna and Paul.

With a gasp of alarm, Joanna rushed to the window, her heart pounding in her chest as she peered into the darkness. What she saw chilled her to the core – a horde of shadowy figures, their twisted forms illuminated by the faint glow of the moon.

"Paul, look!" she exclaimed, her voice trembling with fear as she clutched her husband's arm. "It's them... the creatures from Esmeria! They've found us!"

Paul's eyes widened in horror as he beheld the sight before him, his mind reeling with disbelief. "How is this possible?" he whispered, his voice barely above a hoarse whisper. "We have to protect ourselves, Joanna. We have to--"

Before he could finish his sentence, a sudden crash echoed through the house, followed by the sound of splintering wood. With a cry of alarm, Joanna and Paul sprang into action, their instincts kicking into overdrive as they barricaded themselves in the living room.

As they huddled together, fear gripping their hearts like a vice, Joanna's thoughts turned to her son, thousands of miles away in the distant land of Esmeria. "Oh, Alex," she murmured, her voice choked with emotion. "Please be safe... please come home to us."

Meanwhile, in the mystical realm of Esmeria, Alex and his friends found themselves embroiled in a desperate struggle against the forces of darkness. the threat posed by Zyro and his minions grew ever more dire, their malevolent influence spreading like a shadow across the land.

As they fought valiantly to protect the innocent and thwart Zyro's wicked schemes, a sense of unease gnawed at the back of Alex's mind. He couldn't shake the feeling that something was wrong, that his loved ones were in danger back in the world he had left behind.

"Guys, we need to hurry," Alex urged, his voice tinged with urgency as he glanced at his companions. "I can't shake this feeling that my parents are in trouble. We have to find a way back to Earth, and fast."

Lyra nodded in agreement, her expression grave as she gazed at Alex with concern. "I understand, Alex," she replied, her voice soft yet determined. "We'll find a way to get you home, I promise."

Jix's brow furrowed with worry as he scanned the horizon, his keen senses on high alert for any sign of danger. "We'll need to move quickly and cautiously," he warned, his voice tinged with concern. "Zyro's forces are growing stronger by the minute."

In a cruel twist of fate, the Dark Storm creatures, acting on Zyro's orders, descended upon the bustling streets of London, their twisted forms striking fear into the hearts of its inhabitants. Among their victims was Helen, Alex's beloved girlfriend, whose abduction served as a grim reminder of the lengths to which Zyro would go to exact his revenge.

Marcus and Scarlette, powerless to intervene in the physical realm, could only watch in anguish as Helen was snatched away from the safety of her home. Their hearts ached with the weight of their failure, knowing that they were unable to protect those they cared for most.

But amidst the despair, a glimmer of hope emerged. Through their supernatural connection to the realm of Esmeria, Marcus and Scarlette discovered a newfound ability – the power to traverse the boundaries between worlds. It was a revelation that filled them with both trepidation and determination, for they knew that their journey into Esmeria held the key to unlocking the secrets of their salvation.

Venturing into the mystical realm, Marcus and Scarlette found themselves face to face with an unexpected ally – Dippy's Ghost. Unlike any apparition they had encountered before, Dippy appeared as an angelic being, his ethereal form radiating with an otherworldly light.

"Dippy," Marcus exclaimed, his voice filled with awe and reverence. "What brings you to this realm?"

Dippy's spectral visage shimmered with a sense of purpose as he spoke, his words carrying an air of solemnity. "I come bearing a message of hope," he declared, his voice echoing with an otherworldly resonance. "There is a way to bring you back to life, but it will require the aid of young Alex and a special object hidden within Vesta's palace."

Marcus and Scarlette exchanged a knowing glance, their hearts filled with a renewed sense of purpose. They knew that their path was clear – they must guide Alex on his quest to retrieve the elusive object, for it held the key to their salvation.

Returning to the mortal realm, Marcus and Scarlette appeared to Alex in a dream, their ghostly forms shimmering with an ethereal light. They spoke to him of their plight, of the special object that could bring them back to life, and of the hope that still burned bright within their hearts.

As Alex awoke from his dream, he found himself in the safety of a secluded cave, its walls bathed in the soft glow of moonlight filtering through the entrance. The air was cool and crisp, carrying with it the gentle rustle of leaves from the nearby forest.

Lyra and Jix lay beside him, their forms illuminated by the faint light, their breathing steady and calm as they slept soundly after a long day of adventuring. The cave provided a refuge from the dangers that lurked outside, a temporary sanctuary where they could rest and rejuvenate before continuing their journey.

Outside, the forest whispered secrets to the night, its ancient trees standing sentinel against the darkness. The air was alive with the symphony of nocturnal creatures, their calls echoing through the stillness of the night.

But within the safety of the cave, all was peaceful and serene. The flickering glow of a small fire cast dancing shadows upon the walls, its warmth a comforting presence amidst the cool night air.

tears streaming down his cheeks, he felt a sense of longing for his ghostly friends who had become his confidants and companions in the darkest of times. But amidst the pain of their absence, he found solace in their words of encouragement, in the knowledge that they believed in him and his ability to overcome any obstacle that stood in his way.

As Alex and Lyra made their way towards Jix's lab, their hearts pounded with a mixture of excitement. The final components of the inter-dimensional known as the "self-roaming magical steering" jet were within their grasp.

 they found themselves face to face with the Guardians of the Gardens – formidable creatures resembling giant spikey lizards with razor-sharp teeth and tongues that lashed out with deadly precision. As the creatures spat fireballs and moved with lightning speed, Alex and Lyra knew that they were in for the fight of their lives.

With a grim determination, Alex and Lyra unleashed the power of their upgraded D-ICE Blasters, the icy blasts slicing through the air with a hiss of frost. But the creatures proved to be formidable adversaries, their thick scales providing ample protection against the freezing onslaught.

As the battle raged on, the maze became a chaotic battleground, the air thick with the acrid scent of smoke and the sound of roaring flames. Alex and Lyra fought valiantly, their movements coordinated and precise as they dodged the creatures' relentless attacks.

But despite their best efforts, disaster struck as Lyra found herself cornered by two of the creatures, their fiery breaths hot on her heels. With a cry of alarm, she stumbled backwards, her back hitting the cold stone wall as the creatures closed in for the kill.

"Lyra!" Alex shouted, his voice filled with desperation as he rushed to her aid, his heart pounding in his chest. "Hang on, I'm coming!"

With a burst of speed, Alex lunged forward, his D-ICE Blaster aimed squarely at the creatures' heads. The icy blast struck true, enveloping the creatures in a shimmering cocoon of frost. But even as they froze in place, their fiery breaths still burned bright, melting the ice with alarming speed.

As the creatures began to break free from their icy prison, Jix emerged from the shadows, his own D-ICE Blaster at the ready. With a swift motion, he unleashed a torrent of icy blasts, his aim true as he targeted the creatures' vulnerable spots.

Together, Alex, Lyra, and Jix fought with all their might, their determination unwavering even in the face of seemingly insurmountable odds. With each icy blast, the creatures stumbled and faltered, their movements growing sluggish as the frost crept through their veins.

But just as victory seemed within their grasp, disaster struck once more as the creatures began to rise from the icy depths, their eyes glowing with renewed determination. With a sinking feeling in his heart, Alex knew that the battle was far from over.

"We can't give up now," Lyra exclaimed, her voice filled with determination as she brushed aside the pain of her injuries. "We have to keep fighting, no matter what!"

Jix nodded in agreement, his eyes blazing with fierce resolve. "We've come too far to turn back now," he declared, his voice ringing out with conviction. "Together, we can overcome any obstacle that stands in our way!"

Alex, Lyra, and Jix unleashed a barrage of icy blasts, their combined efforts overwhelming the creatures as they fought tooth and nail for victory and the last of the creatures fell to the ground, defeated but not destroyed and there laying on the ground glistening in the centre of the maze was the magical self roaming steering wheel component.

As our heroes finally escaped the treacherous maze and reached the safety of Jix's lab, a sense of relief washed over them like a wave. With the components in hand, they wasted no time in collaborating with Jix to assemble the otherworldly fighter jet – a marvel of technology and magic combined.

Jix christened the jet the "Knight Jet" in his honour. It was a fitting tribute to the young hero who had fought tirelessly against the forces of darkness, and Alex couldn't help but feel a swell of pride as he prepared to take the helm.

With a deep breath, Alex climbed into the pilot's seat, his hands steady on the controls as he prepared for takeoff. Beside him, Lyra and Jix strapped themselves in, their expressions a mix of excitement and apprehension as they braced themselves for the journey ahead.

As the engines roared to life, the Knight Jet surged forward, hurtling towards the sky with a deafening roar. For a moment, it seemed as though nothing could stop them – but then disaster struck.

With a sudden jolt, the jet malfunctioned, its systems glitching as it careened out of control. Alex fought desperately to regain command, his heart pounding in his chest as he struggled to stabilize their trajectory.

But despite his best efforts, the jet veered off course, hurtling through the fabric of reality itself as it traversed through various dimensions with alarming speed.

With a sense of relief, Alex guided the jet towards their destination, the towering spires of Vesta's palace visible in the distance.

Standing before them, his towering form casting a menacing shadow over the land, was Zyro – the malevolent being whose dark influence had wrought havoc upon Esmeria. With a snarl of rage, he turned to face the approaching jet, his eyes burning with a malevolent fire.

Without hesitation, Alex activated the jet's weapons systems, unleashing a barrage of laser beams towards their formidable foe. But Zyro, fueled by anger and hatred, swiped at the plane with a ferocious swipe of his clawed hand, sending it spiralling towards the earth below.

With a sickening lurch, the Knight Jet crash-landed in a nearby forest, its hull battered and broken from the impact. Inside, our heroes braced themselves for the inevitable, knowing that their journey was far from over – but with courage and determination burning bright in their hearts, they were ready to face whatever challenges lay ahead.

As Alex, Lyra, and Jix emerged from the wreckage of the crashed Knight Jet, a sense of relief washed over them as they realized they had escaped relatively unscathed. Their bodies ached from the impact, but their spirits remained unbroken, fueled by a fierce determination to confront the looming threat of Zyro once and for all.

As Alex surveyed the scene before him, his eyes fell upon the glimmering gold ghost coin lying amidst the wreckage. With a jolt of realization, he remembered the power it held – the power to grant him super strength and flight. Clutching the coin tightly in his hand, he felt a surge of energy coursing through his veins, filling him with newfound confidence and resolve.

Alex activated the ghost coin's power, feeling the exhilarating rush of energy as he soared into the air, leaving Lyra and Jix gazing up at him in awe.

Hovering high above the ground, Alex's eyes narrowed as he locked onto Zyro's towering form, his heart pounding with a mixture of fear and determination. with a roar of defiance, Zyro unleashed a torrent of dark-coloured fire from his gaping maw, the flames licking at the air with an otherworldly intensity. But Alex was prepared – with a swift manoeuvre, he dodged the fiery, rush of wind whipping through his hair as he soared through the sky. "Zyro," Alex's voice echoed with steely resolve, "this ends now. surrender yourself to justice."

Zyro's eyes gleamed with malice as he chuckled darkly. "Foolish human," he snarled, "I will not be bound by your petty notions of justice."

With a flick of his massive claws, Zyro unleashed a barrage of dark fire, engulfing the battlefield in flames. Alex leapt and dodged, his movements fluid and precise, but the inferno raged on, threatening to consume everything in its path.

As the flames danced around him, Alex's thoughts raced.

Where was Helen? She had to be nearby, hidden from Zyro's sight. But in the chaos of battle, finding her would be no easy task.

Meanwhile, Helen crouched behind a crumbling ruin, her heart pounding in her chest. The creatures that served Zyro prowled the area, their sinister forms casting eerie shadows in the flickering firelight. She dared not make a sound, lest they discover her hiding place.

"Where are you, Helen?" Alex's voice echoed in her mind, filled with urgency and concern. "Stay hidden, we'll find you."

Helen clutched her trembling hands together, her breaths shallow and ragged. She prayed silently for Alex's safety, knowing that he faced a formidable opponent in Zyro.

Outside, the battle raged on, each clash of steel and roar of flame echoing through the night. But amidst the chaos, a chilling realization dawned on Helen – the creatures were closing in on her hiding spot.

She pressed herself against the cold stone, willing herself to be invisible. The creatures drew nearer, their guttural growls sending shivers down her spine. With bated breath, she waited, her heart hammering in her chest.

Suddenly, a pair of glowing eyes pierced the darkness, fixing their gaze on her trembling form. Helen's blood ran cold as the creature advanced, its jagged teeth gleaming in the firelight.

"Please," she whispered, her voice barely audible over the roar of battle, "please don't let them find me."

But her pleas fell on deaf ears as the creature lunged forward, its claws outstretched. With a gasp of terror, Helen held her breath, bracing herself for the inevitable capture.

"Helen," Alex shouted, his voice filled with desperation as he lunged forward to protect her. But it was too late – with a swift motion, Zyro's minion seized Helen, his claws digging into her flesh as she cried out in pain.

As he closed in on Zyro, Alex's eyes fell upon a sight that filled him with dread – Helen, held captive in the creature's other hand, her form limp and lifeless, seemingly overcome with fear.

"Let her go, Zyro!" Alex's voice rang out, echoing across the battlefield with a steely determination. "She has nothing to do with this!" Zyro only sneered in response, his eyes gleaming with malice as he tightened his grip on Helen's unconscious form. "She is but a pawn in our game, little hero," he growled, his voice dripping with venom. "And you are nothing but an inconvenience."

With a cry of rage, Alex launched himself at Zyro, his fists clenched with righteous fury as he unleashed a barrage of blows upon the creature's grotesque visage. Each punch landed with a resounding thud, the force of Alex's super strength driving Zyro back with each angry blow.

Zyro, fueled by his malevolent power, refused to go down without a fight. With a roar of defiance, he lashed out at Alex with a savage swipe of his clawed hand, the force of the blow sending Alex reeling through the air.

As he struggled to regain his balance, Alex felt a surge of determination coursing through his veins. He would not let Zyro's tyranny go unchecked – not while there was still hope for Esmeria and its people.

As the dark storm monsters continued their relentless assault on the suburban streets of London, Paul and Joanna Knight found themselves facing an unexpected dilemma. With fear gnawing at their hearts, they rushed into Alex's room, their eyes falling upon the familiar sight of his cupboard where the D-Blasters lay hidden.

With a mixture of apprehension, Paul and Joanna each took hold of a blaster, their hands trembling with anticipation as they prepared to face the creatures that lurked outside.

# CHAPTER NINE

## DARK STORM IN LONDON

With a grin of excitement, Paul aimed at one of the creatures, his laughter mingling with Joanna's as they unleashed a barrage of blasts, sending the dark storm monsters scattering in all directions. For a moment, the weight of their worries was lifted, replaced by a sense of exhilaration and adrenaline-fueled fun.

Paul and Joanna couldn't shake the feeling that something was wrong – that their son, Alex, was in grave danger far away in the mystical realm of Esmeria.

Turning their attention to Alex's room, Paul's gaze fell upon an ancient book nestled amongst his belongings – a relic from a time long forgotten. he reached for the book, his fingers tracing the intricate patterns that adorned its weathered cover.

"Paul, what are you doing?" Joanna's voice broke through the silence, her eyes filled with concern as she watched her husband's every move. "We need to focus on Alex – he's the one in danger, not us."

But Paul's resolve remained unwavering as he opened the book, his eyes scanning the pages in search of answers. As the ancient words danced before his eyes, he felt a surge of power coursing through his veins – a power that could help them reach their son in his time of need.

With a flick of his wrist, Paul recited the incantation written within the pages of the ancient tome, his voice echoing with a strange, otherworldly resonance. And in an instant, a swirling vortex of light erupted before them, opening a portal to the distant realm of Esmeria.

As the portal shimmered into existence, Alex and his friends stared in astonishment, their hearts filled with a mixture of surprise and apprehension. But before they could react, Paul stepped through the portal, his determination driving him forward as he sought to aid his son in the battle against the forces of darkness.

"Paul, no!" Alex cried out, his voice filled with alarm as he watched his stepfather's bold move. "You shouldn't be here – it's too dangerous!" "I have to do this Alex, I haven't got much to lose!" Paul protested.

"What do you mean?" asked Alex taken back. "Alex..I'm…I'm sorry, your mother and I were waiting for the right time to tell you" his stepfather shot back sorrowfully fighting back tears. "but…I…I have cancer. With not much time left" he continued "I would still risk my life if it mean protecting you, son and it would be worth the risk" he smiled warmly.

"Dad! You don't have to do this!" Alex yelled aggressively wiping tears streaming from his face.

But Paul paid no heed to Alex's protests, his eyes locked on the towering figure of Zyro as he raised the D-Blaster in his hand. With a sense of grim determination, he aimed at the malevolent being, his finger poised on the trigger.

But before he could unleash the blast, Zyro moved with lightning speed, his clawed hand slashing through the air with deadly precision. And in an instant, Paul's world went dark as Zyro's attack struck true, sending him crashing to the ground in a lifeless heap.

The air filled with the sound of Alex's anguished screams as he watched helplessly, his heart breaking at the sight of his stepfather's sacrifice. At that moment, he realized the true cost of their battle against the forces of darkness – a cost paid in blood, and in the lives of those they held most dear.

As Zyro stood triumphantly before Alex and Jix, his voice booming with a sense of authority and superiority, a hush fell over the battlefield. His dark form loomed large against the backdrop of the crumbling palace, his eyes gleaming with an otherworldly intensity as he addressed the gathered crowd.

"People of Esmeria," Zyro's voice echoed across the land, carrying with it a sense of ominous foreboding. "You stand on the precipice of a new era – an era of darkness and despair. But it does not have to be this way."

With a sweeping gesture, Zyro extended his clawed hand towards the dying Vesta, her form flickering with fading light. "Your beloved ruler lies on the brink of death, her power waning with each passing moment," he proclaimed. "But fear not, for I offer you salvation – salvation through submission."

A murmur of uncertainty rippled through the crowd as Zyro's words hung in the air, their implications weighing heavily on the hearts of the gathered Esmerians. But before anyone could respond, Lyra stepped forward, her gaze locked with Zyro's as she made her decision known. "I choose to stand with Zyro," she declared, her voice filled with conviction. "He offers us power, stability, and the promise of a better future. Why should we fight against him when we can join him and embrace our destiny?"

The stunned silence that followed was deafening, as Alex and Jix struggled to comprehend the magnitude of Lyra's betrayal. How could she turn against them, against everything they had fought for?

But as Lyra joined forces with Zyro, her allegiance shifting in the blink of an eye, Alex and Jix knew that they could no longer afford to hesitate. With a heavy heart, Alex raised his D-ICE Blaster, his hands trembling with a mixture of anger and disbelief.

"We cannot let Zyro's lies deceive us," Jix proclaimed, his voice ringing out with a sense of urgency. "We must stand united against the darkness that threatens to consume us all. Esmeria is our home, and we will defend it to the last."

Jix turned to the gathered citizens of Esmeria, his words igniting a spark of hope within their hearts. Together, they raised their voices in defiance, determined to resist Zyro's tyranny and protect their land from destruction.

The dark storm army descended upon the unsuspecting citizens with a ferocity that shook the very foundations of Esmeria, their relentless assault pushing the defenders to their limits.

As the battle raged on and the strain of using his ghost powers began to take its toll, Alex felt a subtle shift within himself. A faint tingling sensation swept through his body, accompanied by a strange feeling of unease that settled in the pit of his stomach.

With a furrowed brow, Alex glanced down at his hands, noting with a sense of trepidation the subtle changes that were beginning to take place. His features seemed to blur and shift ever so slightly, a strange sensation washing over him as he felt a presence stirring deep within his soul.

And then, he heard it – a voice, soft and ethereal, echoing in the recesses of his mind like a whisper carried on the wind. "Hello, Alex," it said, its tone both familiar and unsettling. "Did you miss me?"

Alex's heart skipped a beat as he recognized the voice – his alter ego, the enigmatic entity known as Lexa. For years, she had been a constant presence in his life, a manifestation of his innermost desires and fears.

Alex clenched his fists, fighting to maintain control over his thoughts as he faced the manifestation of his innermost desires and fears. "Not today, Lexa," he responded, his voice tinged with determination. "I have a battle to fight, and I won't let you stand in my way."

But Lexa's laughter danced on the edges of his consciousness, her words laced with a tantalizing allure. "Oh, Alex, you can't deny me forever," she taunted, her voice dripping with malice.

"I am a part of you, woven into the very fabric of your being. You cannot escape me."

Anger surged within Alex's chest, a fierce fire burning in his eyes as he pushed back against the invasive thoughts that threatened to overwhelm him. "I am not defined by you, Lexa," he declared, his voice ringing with conviction. "I am my person, with my hopes and dreams. I won't let you control me any longer."

But Lexa's laughter only grew louder, his presence looming larger in his mind with each passing moment. "You can fight all you want, Alex, but you cannot deny the truth," he whispered, his words a haunting echo in the depths of his soul. "I am a part of you, and I will always be."

Frustration welled up inside Alex as he struggled to push back against the relentless onslaught of doubt and uncertainty. "No," he shouted, his voice echoing through the empty expanse of his mind. "I refuse to let you dictate my fate. I am in control here, not you."

For a moment, there was silence, broken only by the sound of Alex's ragged breathing as he wrestled with his inner demons.

"I am Alex Knight," he declared, his voice ringing with conviction. "And I will not be defined by my past or my fears. I will forge my path, no matter what obstacles may stand in my way."

As Alex struggled against the relentless taunts of Lexa, his resolve wavered for a moment, the weight of his inner turmoil threatening to drag him down into despair. But deep within his heart, a spark of determination flickered to life, fueled by the memory of those he held dear and the unyielding spirit of defiance that burned within him.

"I must save Helen, my friends, and Esmeria," Alex whispered to himself, his voice a defiant mantra against the darkness that threatened to consume him. "I've come this far, and I can do this."

Alex summoned every ounce of strength and courage within him, pushing back against the suffocating grip of doubt. As he focused his thoughts on the task at hand, Alex soared through the palace corridors, his heart pounding with anticipation as he drew closer to his destination. As he burst through the ornate double doors leading to Vesta's chamber, he was met with a scene of solemnity and sorrow.

Vesta lay upon a gilded bed, her form shrouded in the dim light that filtered through the stained glass windows. Surrounding her were her loyal guards and servants, their faces etched with concern as they tended to their ailing ruler with gentle hands and solemn expressions.

Approaching her bedside, Alex felt a surge of empathy welling up within him as he gazed upon Vesta's weakened form. Despite her regal bearing and air of authority, she appeared fragile and vulnerable in her current state, a shadow of her former self.

"Vesta," Alex spoke softly, his voice as he addressed the ailing ruler. "I've come to help you. What can I do?"

Vesta's weary eyes flickered open at the sound of his voice, a faint smile tugging at the corners of her lips. "Alex," she greeted him warmly, her voice barely above a whisper. "Thank you for coming. There is something you must do – a task of great importance."

Drawing closer to her bedside, Alex listened intently as Vesta imparted her wisdom, her words carrying the weight of centuries of wisdom and experience. "In the depths of the palace dungeon lies a secret – a weapon powerful enough to defeat Zyro and restore balance to Esmeria," she explained, her voice filled with conviction. "You must retrieve it and use it to vanquish the darkness that threatens our world."

Alex nodded solemnly, his determination burning brighter than ever as he vowed to carry out Vesta's wishes. "I won't let you down, Vesta," he promised, his voice ringing with resolve. "I will do whatever it takes to save Esmeria and restore you to full strength."

Alex turned and made his way towards the palace dungeon, his heart filled with a fierce determination to confront the challenges that lay ahead and emerge victorious against the forces of darkness that threatened to engulf them all.

As Alex descended into the depths of Vesta's palace dungeon, the air grew heavy with an oppressive stillness, broken only by the faint echoes of his footsteps as they reverberated against the cold stone walls. His heart pounded in his chest, The dungeon stretched out before him like a shadow, its twisting corridors shrouded in mystery and danger. he pressed forward in search of the powerful artefact that would aid him in his quest.

As he moved into the dungeon, Alex's keen eyes scanned his surroundings for any signs of danger. Booby traps lay in wait around every corner, their mechanisms cunningly concealed to ensnare the unwary traveller. But Alex's sharp instincts and quick reflexes served him well, allowing him to evade each trap with skill and precision.

But it was not just trapped that stood in his way – the dungeon was also home to a variety of otherworldly creatures, their grotesque forms lurking in the shadows, ready to strike at a moment's notice. Giant insects scuttled across the floor, their chittering cries echoing off the damp stone walls as they sought to defend their territory from intruders.

As Alex approached the pedestal in the centre of the chamber, he noticed a faint inscription etched into the stone tablet resting upon it. The guardian of the artefact, a spectral figure cloaked in shadows, emerged from the darkness, its voice echoing with an otherworldly resonance.

"Welcome, seeker, to the Chamber of Trials. Only those who prove themselves worthy may lay claim to the artefact that lies within." The Guardian proclaimed

Alex squared his shoulders, his determination shining in his eyes. "I am ready to face whatever challenges you present," he declared.

"Very well, Guardian said. Let us begin with a test of wit. Answer me this riddle:

*'I speak without a mouth and hear without ears. I have nobody,*

*but I come alive with the wind. What am I?'"*

Alex furrowed his brow, pondering the riddle with intense focus. Suddenly, realization dawned upon him like a burst of sunlight piercing through the darkness.

*"A voice,"* he said confidently. *"The answer is a voice."*

"Correct," the guardian intoned, its voice tinged with approval. "You have passed the first trial. But the challenges ahead will only grow more difficult."

"Indeed," the Guardian continued, "But before we proceed to the next trial, let us dwell on the significance of your answer. A voice, yes, a manifestation of intangible power, capable of stirring emotions, instilling fear, or igniting hope."

Alex nodded, absorbing the weight of the Guardian's words. "It's fascinating how something so immaterial can wield such influence," he remarked, his mind racing with newfound insights.

"Indeed," the Guardian echoed, its gaze piercing through Alex's thoughts. "But remember, seeker, just as a voice can inspire greatness, it can also harbour deceit. In the trials ahead, discernment will be your greatest ally."

"As you embark on this journey," the Guardian intoned, "keep in mind that the artefact you seek holds not only power but also the wisdom of those who came before you. Its secrets are bound to the fabric of time, waiting for one worthy enough to unravel them."

Alex's curiosity surged at the mention of ancient wisdom,

envisioning the possibility of uncovering truths long forgotten.

"Tell me, Guardian," he inquired, "what awaits me in the next trial?"

The Guardian's eyes gleamed with enigmatic knowledge, hinting at the mysteries yet to be revealed. "Patience, seeker," it replied cryptically. "For now, rest your mind and replenish your spirit. The journey ahead will test not only your intellect but also your resilience."

With a nod of understanding, Alex settled into a contemplative silence, preparing himself for the challenges that lay ahead. In the Chamber of Trials, where time seemed to stand still, he embraced the uncertainty of the path before him, knowing that each step would bring him closer to the artefact and the enlightenment it promised.

"Indeed," the Guardian mused, its voice echoing with ancient wisdom. "The power of the spoken word transcends mere sound; it carries the weight of history, the resonance of truth, and the echo of destiny."

Alex listened intently, his gaze fixed on the enigmatic figure before him. "It's incredible to think about the impact a simple voice can have," he remarked, his mind racing with a newfound appreciation for the subtleties of communication.

"Ah, but do not be deceived by its simplicity," the Guardian cautioned, its eyes gleaming with insight. "For within the whispers of the wind lies the potential for both liberation and manipulation."

A shiver ran down Alex's spine as he considered the

Guardian's words. "So, the trials ahead will test not only my wit but also my discernment," he surmised, a sense of determination burning within him.

"Indeed," the Guardian affirmed, its voice a solemn reminder of the challenges yet to come. "But fear not, seeker, for within you lies the strength to navigate the intricacies of truth and falsehood."

As the weight of the Guardian's words settled upon him, Alex felt a surge of resolve coursing through his veins. "I am ready," he declared, his voice ringing with conviction. "Ready to face whatever trials await me and claim the artefact that lies within this chamber."

A knowing smile graced the Guardian's lips as it nodded in approval. "Then let us proceed," it said, gesturing toward the shadowy depths of the chamber. "The journey ahead will be arduous, but with courage and determination, you shall emerge victorious."

With a deep breath, Alex stepped forward, his heart pounding with anticipation.

As the stone tablet slid aside, revealing the next phase of the puzzle, Alex prepared himself for the next test.

Moving to the next challenge, "What must I do to proceed?" he asked, turning to the guardian for guidance.

"To overcome this trial, you must navigate the maze of symbols and reach the other side. But beware, for the path is treacherous, and one wrong step could lead to your downfall." The guardian responded

With a nod of understanding, Alex set to work, his eyes scanning the maze for any discernible pattern or route to follow.

As Alex meticulously traced his way through the maze, the guardian watched in silence, its gaze unreadable behind the veil of shadows. With each twist and turn, Alex's confidence grew, his determination driving him forward despite the daunting challenge before him.

Finally, after what felt like an eternity of careful navigation, Alex emerged victorious, reaching the other side of the maze unscathed.

"Impressive," the guardian murmured, its voice filled with grudging respect. "You have proven yourself to be a worthy challenger indeed."

With a sense of accomplishment, Alex turned his attention to the artefact that lay within reach, as he reached out to grasp the artefact, the guardian's spectral form shimmered with a faint light, indicating its approval of his progress.

"You have shown both intellect and skill, seeker. But one final challenge remains before you may claim the artefact as your own." The Guardian said.

Alex paused, his hand hovering just inches away from the gleaming crystal sword/staff.

"What must I do to prove myself worthy of this final trial?" he inquired, his voice steady despite the anticipation coursing through his veins.

"You must demonstrate your mastery of the elements," the guardian replied cryptically. "Only then will the artefact recognize you as its rightful wielder."

With a determined nod, Alex prepared himself for the ultimate test, steeling his resolve as he braced for whatever challenge awaited him.

Suddenly, the chamber began to tremble, the air crackling with energy as a series of elemental symbols materialized before him, each representing a different aspect of nature – fire, water, earth, and air.

"Choose wisely, the Guardian whispered, for the element you select will determine the nature of your final trial."

Alex surveyed the symbols before him, weighing his options carefully as he considered the strengths and weaknesses of each element.

# CHAPTER TEN

## "EMBERS OF HOPE: A SAGA OF FIRE, FURY, AND TRIUMPH"

"I choose fire," he declared, his voice resolute as he made his decision.

As he spoke the words, the chamber erupted into a blaze of flames, engulfing the room in a fiery inferno that danced and flickered with chaotic energy.

"Your choice has been made," the guardian intoned, its voice echoing above the roar of the flames. "Now, you must prove your mastery over the fire if you wish to claim the artefact." The Guardian echoed

With a deep breath, Alex stepped forward into the heart of the inferno, his body bathed in the searing heat as he summoned forth his inner strength.

with a triumphant roar, he emerged from the flames unscathed, the power of fire coursing through his veins like a raging wildfire.

"You have surpassed all expectations, seeker," the guardian proclaimed, its voice filled with awe and reverence. "The artefact is yours to wield, for you have proven yourself worthy of its power."

With a sense of profound gratitude, Alex reached out and claimed the artefact as his own, feeling its power surge through him like a torrential wave.

As he held the artefact aloft, a sense of purpose filled his heart, knowing that he had triumphed over adversity and emerged victorious.

As Alex stood in the chamber, his grip tightened around the powerful ancient crystal staff, its silver handle cool against his palm. The blue jewel at the bottom gleamed with an otherworldly allure, seeming to pulse with the very heartbeat of the realm.

With a deep breath, he whispered, "Thank you, Dippy, for guiding me in spirit,".

With a flick of his wrist, Alex retrieved the ghost coin from his pocket, its surface smooth beneath his thumb. As he rubbed it, a gentle warmth spread from the coin, enveloping him with spectral energy. With a surge of power, he ascended once more, propelled upward by the unseen force that had aided him throughout his journey.

High above, amidst the swirling chaos of the cavern, Zyro loomed like a shadowy titan, his form wreathed in flickering flames. As Alex soared toward him, the glowing shield held aloft, he could feel the intensity of the creature's malevolent gaze boring into him.

Zyro's roar echoed through the chamber, a deafening symphony of rage and fury. Flames erupted from his maw, a searing torrent aimed directly at Alex. With a swift movement, Alex raised the shield, its surface shimmering with a protective aura as it absorbed the brunt of the fiery assault.

As Zyro lunged forward, jaws snapping hungrily, Alex met his advance head-on. With a deft manoeuvre, he sidestepped the creature's attack, the razor-sharp edge of the crystal staff gleaming as it arced toward Zyro's chest. With a resounding impact, the blade found its mark, burying itself deep within the creature's flesh with a sickening crunch.

A roar of agony echoed through the chamber as Zyro staggered backwards, his strength waning with each passing moment. As the dark storm creatures that had surrounded him began to falter and fade, Alex pressed his advantage, his strikes relentless and precise as he delivered blow after blow upon his wounded foe.

And then, with a final, decisive thrust, Alex drove the crystal staff deep into Zyro's heart, its radiant energy pulsating intensity. With a deafening roar, the creature collapsed to the ground, its form dissipating into nothingness as the shadows that had plagued the land began to recede.

As Alex clashed with Zyro, Helen, Alex's beloved girlfriend, found herself ensnared in Zyro's grip, her screams lost amidst the combat. With a primal roar of rage, Alex lunged forward, his heart pounding in his chest as he fought to reach her before it was too late.

With a mighty effort, Zyro released his hold on Helen, sending her tumbling through the air towards the unforgiving ground below.

Alex darted forward, his arms outstretched to catch her before she could meet her doom.

As Helen's unconscious form came crashing into his embrace, Alex felt a surge of relief flood through him, his heart pounding with the intensity of their near miss. Cradling her gently in his arms, he whispered words of reassurance, his voice a soothing balm against the turmoil that surrounded them.

As Alex clasped Helen tightly to his chest, his breath ragged with adrenaline, he murmured to her, his voice trembling with emotion. "Helen, my love, are you alright? Can you hear me?"

Helen stirred slightly in his arms, her eyelids fluttering open as she struggled to focus. "Alex?" she whispered, her voice barely audible over the din of battle. "What... what happened?"

"You're safe now, Helen," Alex replied, his voice filled with relief. "Zyro had you in his grasp, but I've got you. You're going to be okay."

Helen's eyes widened with sudden realization, a shiver coursing through her body as the memory of Zyro's menacing grip flooded back to her. "Zyro... he was so strong," she gasped, her voice trembling. "I thought I was done for."

Alex tightened his hold on her, his gaze fierce as he scanned their surroundings for any sign of their adversary. "He won't hurt you again, Helen. I won't let him."

"But Alex," Helen murmured, her brow furrowed with worry, "what if he comes back? What if he tries to take me again?"

Alex's jaw clenched with determination, his eyes ablaze with fierce protectiveness. "Then he'll have to answer to me," he declared, his voice steely with resolve. "I'll never let anyone harm you, Helen. Not now, not ever."

Helen gazed up at him, her heart swelling with gratitude and love. "Thank you, Alex," she whispered, her voice soft but fervent. "I don't know what I'd do without you."

Alex brushed a gentle kiss against her forehead, his touch tender and reassuring. "You'll never have to find out, Helen," he vowed, his voice filled with unwavering devotion. "I'll always be here for you, no matter what."

Vesta, her powers reignited by the flames of determination and hope, unleashed a torrent of energy against Zyro, her attacks weaving through the air with lethal precision. With each strike, the darkness that had gripped the land faltered, its hold weakening beneath the onslaught of her formidable abilities.

As Vesta's powers surged forth, illuminating the battlefield with their fiery brilliance, Zyro staggered backwards, his expression a mixture of surprise and determination. "Impressive, Vesta," he growled, his voice carrying a sinister edge. "But do you truly believe you can defeat me?"

Vesta's eyes blazed with determination as she narrowed her focus on her adversary. "I will not rest until the darkness you've brought upon this land is vanquished," she declared, her voice ringing out with unwavering resolve.

Zyro chuckled darkly, his lips curling into a malevolent grin. "Such bravery," he sneered. "But bravery alone will not save you." With a swift motion, he conjured a barrier of shadow to deflect Vesta's next onslaught of energy.

Zyro's laughter echoed across the battlefield, the sound sending shivers down Vesta's spine. "Belief can be a powerful weapon," he admitted, his tone laced with malice. "But it can also be a weakness. And yours will be your downfall."

Vesta's jaw clenched as she summoned even more power, the flames of her determination burning brighter than ever. "We'll see about that," she retorted, her voice dripping with defiance. "Because as long as there's even a glimmer of hope, the darkness will never triumph." With a fierce cry, she unleashed another wave of energy, determined to prove Zyro wrong and bring an end to the tyranny that threatened to consume their world.

As Vesta's powers surged forth, illuminating the battlefield with their fiery brilliance, Zyro staggered backwards, his expression a mixture of surprise and determination. "Impressive, Vesta," he growled, his voice carrying a sinister edge. "But do you truly believe you can defeat me?"

Vesta's eyes blazed with determination as she narrowed her focus on her adversary. "I will not rest until the darkness you've brought upon this land is vanquished," she declared, her voice ringing out with unwavering resolve.

Zyro chuckled darkly, his lips curling into a malevolent grin. "Such bravery," he sneered. "But bravery alone will not save you." With a swift motion, he conjured a barrier of shadow to deflect Vesta's next onslaught of energy.

Zyro's laughter echoed across the battlefield, the sound sending shivers down Vesta's spine. "Belief can be a powerful weapon," he admitted, his tone laced with malice. "But it can also be a weakness. And yours will be your downfall."

Vesta's jaw clenched as she summoned even more power, the flames of her determination burning brighter than ever. "We'll see about that," she retorted, her voice dripping with defiance. "Because as long as there's even a glimmer of hope, the darkness will never triumph." With a fierce cry, she unleashed another wave of energy, determined to prove Zyro wrong and bring an end to the tyranny that threatened to consume their world.

Together, Alex and Vesta fought side by side, their combined strength and determination a force to be reckoned with. With a final, decisive blow, Vesta unleashed her full power against Zyro, the force of her attack shattering the creature's defences and leaving it vulnerable to defeat.

As Zyro crumbled beneath the weight of Vesta's assault, a sense of victory swept through the chamber, its echoes reverberating with the cheers of the emboldened citizens of Esmeria. But amidst the celebration, a new threat emerged – Lyra, once a beacon of light, now corrupted by darkness and wielding its power with ruthless efficiency.

Lyra led the dark storm creatures in a desperate bid to reclaim their lost ground, their sinister forms twisting and contorting with malice. But the citizens of Esmeria, emboldened by Alex's bravery and Vesta's leadership, stood firm against the encroaching tide, their determination unyielding as they fought to defend their home.

And as the last of the dark storm creatures fell, defeated at last by the combined efforts of Jix and the valiant defenders of Esmeria, a sense of peace settled over the land once more.

As the final echoes of battle faded into the distance, a profound sense of loss lingered in the air, tempered only by the flickering embers of hope that burned bright within the hearts of Esmeria's defenders. Amidst the smouldering ruins of their once beautiful city, Alex stood with Helen by his side, his heart heavy with grief for those who had fallen in the fight against darkness.

Vesta, after regaining is power restate Dippy, Marcus, Scarlette .

"Dippy, Marcus, Scarlette," she called out, her voice cutting through the tumult of battle. "Rise once more, not as you were, but as something greater!"

A shimmering light enveloped the fallen trio, lifting them from the ground as if they were weightless feathers. Marcus's eyes fluttered open first, followed by Scarlette's and then Dippy's. But dippy forms was different now, bathed in a celestial glow that spoke of newfound power.

"D-Dippy? What... what's happening?" Marcus stammered, bewildered by the transformation.

Scarlette blinked, her gaze darting around as she took in her surroundings. "Vesta, is that you? What did you do?"

Vesta's expression softened with relief as she met their bewildered gazes. "I've brought you back, for we have a battle to win."

Dippy floated upward, his form pulsating with ethereal energy. "I... I feel different, Vesta. Powerful. What do you need from us?"

A smile tugged at Vesta's lips as she regarded her reinvigorated companions. "We fight together, as one. Let the light within guide us to victory!"

But just as despair threatened to overwhelm him, a glimmer of light pierced through the darkness, illuminating the chamber with its radiant glow. And there, standing before him in a form more magnificent than he could have ever imagined, was Dippy – no longer a mere app, but a celestial being of pure light and grace.

"Dippy," Alex whispered, his voice choked with emotion as he beheld the angelic figure before him. "Is it you?"

The angelic form of Dippy smiled warmly, its presence suffusing the chamber with a sense of peace and serenity. "Yes, Alex," it replied its voice a melodic harmony that resonated deep within his soul. "I have been reborn, not as an app, but as a guardian of light, entrusted with guiding and protecting those who seek the path of righteousness."

Tears welled in Alex's eyes with a big surprise as he reached out to embrace his dear friend Marcus and Scarlette once more, his heart overflowing with gratitude for the miracle that had brought Dippy, Marcus and Scarlette once more back into his life. As they stood together, surrounded by the remnants of battle, a sense of hope blossomed within Alex's heart, driving away the shadows of despair that had threatened to consume him.

As the battle raged on between the Ice-Blasters and the menacing creatures, Vesta stood at the heart of the chaos, her hands glowing with a radiant energy. With a determined look in her eyes, she focused her powers on bringing back her friends.

With renewed determination, the trio joined Vesta on the battle field. dippy angelic forms emanating a radiant aura that bolstered the spirits of their allies. Together, they would face the darkness and emerge triumphant, united in purpose and strength. As their fallen comrades were laid to rest amidst the ashes of their once-proud city, Alex and Helen stood side by side, their hearts heavy with grief for the loss of those they had loved and lost.

As the days passed and Esmeria began to rebuild in the wake of devastation, Alex found himself haunted by the absence of his father, whose life had been claimed by the darkness that had threatened to consume them all. Though he longed for his father's presence, he knew in his heart that his time had come, his sacrifice a necessary step in the battle against evil.

And so, as Alex stood at his father's graveside, tears streaming down his face, he whispered a final farewell to the man who had shaped him into the person he had become. "Rest in peace, Dad," he murmured, his voice choked with emotion. "You may be gone, but your memory will live on in my heart forever."

Helen, her grief mirrored in her eyes, wrapped her arms around

Alex, offering him comfort and solace in his darkest hour. "I'm here for you, Alex," she whispered, her voice trembling with emotion. "We'll get through this together."

Alex and Helen knew that they would emerge from the darkness stronger and more resilient than ever before.

And as they looked towards the future with hope and optimism, they vowed to never forget the sacrifices that had been made in the name of freedom and justice, their spirits united in a bond that could never be broken. For in the face of adversity, they had proven that love, courage, and the indomitable human spirit would always prevail.

As the dust settled, a heavy silence hung over the battlefield, broken only by the soft rustle of leaves stirred by the gentle breeze. Alex and his companions cautiously made their way through the wreckage, their eyes scanning the aftermath of the intense battle. Amidst the debris and fallen soldiers, they stumbled upon a startling discovery - the real Lyra, lying unconscious amidst the bushes of the Esmerian forest.

With a gasp, Alex rushed to her side, his heart pounding with a mixture of fear and relief. "Lyra!" he called out, his voice trembling with worry as he gently shook her shoulder. "Lyra, can you hear me?"

Slowly, as if emerging from a deep slumber, Lyra stirred, her eyelids fluttering open to reveal the vibrant green of her eyes, clouded with confusion. "What... what happened?" she murmured, her voice barely above a whisper.

"It's alright, Lyra," Alex reassured her, his voice soft but urgent. "You were unconscious. The imposter, who posed as you, was a follower of Ruok. They caused chaos, but we managed to stop them."

Lyra's brow furrowed in disbelief, her mind struggling to grasp the gravity of the situation. "An imposter?" she echoed, her voice trembling with disbelief. "But how..."

With a heavy heart, Alex recounted the events that had transpired - from the ambush orchestrated by Zyro to the imposter's deceitful actions. His words painted a vivid picture of betrayal and danger, each detail etched into the fabric of their memories.

As he spoke, Lyra's expression shifted from confusion to understanding, a flicker of anger dancing in the depths of her gaze. "So, King Ruok is still a threat," she concluded, her voice laced with determination. "We must remain vigilant. He will return, and we must be prepared to face him."

Alex nodded solemnly, his resolve hardened by the weight of their shared burden. Together, they would stand against the darkness, united in their determination to protect Esmeria and its people from any who sought to harm them.

As the chaos of battle subsided, Esmeria gradually began to return to a semblance of normalcy. The once bustling streets, now scarred by the recent conflict, slowly filled with the sounds of rebuilding and restoration. Amidst the efforts to repair the damage wrought by the Dark Storm, Vesta, the leader of Esmeria, sought out Alex and his companions to express her gratitude for their bravery and sacrifice.

Vesta approached them, her eyes reflecting the weight of the recent events. "Alex, my friends," she began, her voice tinged with both sorrow and gratitude, "I cannot thank you enough for what you have done. You have saved Esmeria from the clutches of darkness, and for that, we are forever in your debt."

She paused, her gaze shifting to Lyra, a mixture of regret and admiration evident in her eyes. "Lyra," she continued, her voice softening with sincerity, "you were right. I should have listened to your warning. You saw the danger looming, and yet I failed to heed your words."

Lyra nodded, her expression tinged with a bittersweet sense of validation. "It's alright, Vesta," she replied, her voice gentle but firm. "What matters now is that we stand together, united against any threat that may come our way."

Vesta's eyes glistened with unshed tears as she reached into her pocket, retrieving a small pouch filled with shimmering jewels. "As a token of our gratitude," she said, her voice choked with emotion, "please accept this humble reward. It is but a small gesture compared to the magnitude of your bravery, but I hope it serves as a reminder of Esmeria's eternal gratitude."

Alex and his friends accepted the gift with humility, their hearts heavy with the weight of their recent losses. As they stood together in a moment of silence, mourning the death of Alex's stepfather and the countless Esmerian victims who had lost their lives to the Dark Storm, a sense of solemn solidarity washed over them.

In the quietude of that moment, amidst the echoes of the past and the hopes for the future, they found strength in each other's presence, knowing that together, they would overcome whatever challenges lay ahead, united in their determination to protect Esmeria and its people from any who sought to harm them.

Vesta's voice trembled with emotion as she addressed Alex and his companions. "Alex, my friends," she began, her eyes brimming with gratitude and sorrow. "I cannot express enough how grateful we are for your bravery. You have saved Esmeria from the clutches of darkness, and for that, we owe you a debt we can never fully repay."

Alex nodded, his own emotions raw from the recent events. "We did what we had to do," he replied, his voice tinged with weariness. "But we couldn't have done it without your guidance, Vesta. You've been a beacon of strength for us all."

Vesta's gaze softened as she turned to Lyra, a hint of regret in her eyes. "Lyra," she said, her voice gentle but remorseful, "you were right all along. I should have listened to your warning about the impending danger. I failed you, and for that, I am deeply sorry."

Lyra placed a comforting hand on Vesta's shoulder, her expression filled with understanding. "It's alright, Vesta," she reassured her, her voice soft but resolute. "What matters now is that we stand together, united against any threat that may come our way."

Vesta nodded, her gratitude evident as she reached into her

pocket, retrieving a small pouch filled with shimmering jewels. "As a token of our appreciation," she said, her voice trembling with emotion, "please accept this humble reward. It is but a small gesture compared to the magnitude of your bravery, but I hope it serves as a reminder of Esmeria's eternal gratitude."

Alex and his friends accepted the gift with humility, their hearts heavy with the weight of their recent losses. As they stood together in a moment of silence, mourning the death of Alex's stepfather and the countless Esmerian victims who had lost their lives to the Dark Storm, a sense of solemn solidarity washed over them.

as Alex and his companions stood in a circle around the lifeless form of Alex's stepfather. Helen, Alex's new girlfriend, stepped forward, her heart aching for him, and gently clasped his hand in hers.

"Alex," she whispered, her voice barely audible above the gentle breeze rustling through the trees, "I'm here for you."

Alex turned to Helen, his eyes reflecting a mixture of gratitude and pain. "Thank you, Helen," he murmured, his voice thick with emotion. "Your support means the world to me."

Feeling the weight of the moment, Helen leaned in and pressed a tender kiss on Alex's cheek, a silent gesture of comfort and love. In response, Alex's lips met hers in a soft, heartfelt kiss, a wordless expression of appreciation and affection amidst their shared grief.

In the distance, Marcus and Scarlette stood together, their

hands intertwined, their silhouettes etched against the fading light of the setting sun. Their hearts heavy with grief, they shared a silent moment of remembrance before turning to join Alex and Helen.

"I miss him," Marcus confessed, his voice trembling with emotion. "He was like a father to me."

Scarlette nodded, her eyes glistening with unshed tears. "He was a good man," she agreed, her voice soft with sorrow. "We owe him so much."

As Alex squeezed Helen's hand tightly, drawing strength from her presence, memories of his stepfather flooded his mind. Each memory was a poignant reminder of the love and guidance he had received.

"He always believed in me," Alex murmured, his voice barely more than a whisper. "I just wish I could have told him one last time how much he meant to me."

Helen wrapped her arms around Alex, offering him solace as they shared a tender embrace. "He knew, Alex," she reassured him, her voice a whisper against his ear. "He knew."

Meanwhile, Marcus gently wiped away a tear from Scarlette's cheek before leaning down to kiss her forehead, a silent vow of support and solidarity in their shared grief.

In the tranquil embrace of the forest, the group stood together in silent reverence. The setting sun cast long shadows across the forest floor, bathing them in a warm golden light as they bowed their heads in a silent prayer for their lost loved one.

Amidst the beauty of nature and the echoes of their shared sorrow, they found comfort in each other's presence, knowing that though their loved one may be gone, his memory would live on in their hearts forever.

It was a cool afternoon when Lucas made his way to the small park on the outskirts of town. The sun cast long shadows across the playground, and the gentle rustle of leaves filled the air. Lucas hesitated at the entrance, his heart heavy with the weight of what he had to do.

Meanwhile, Alex sat on a weathered bench near the edge of the park, lost in thought as he watched the children playing nearby. His mind was still reeling from the events of the past few weeks, and he longed for a moment of peace amidst the chaos.

As Lucas approached the park, he spotted Alex sitting alone on the bench. With each step, his resolve grew stronger, though his nerves threatened to betray him. Finally, he reached the bench where Alex sat, his heart pounding in his chest.

"Alex," Lucas called out, his voice wavering with uncertainty.

Alex turned to see Lucas standing before him, his expression a mix of surprise and curiosity. He had expected to see Lucas in a different setting, perhaps on a crowded street or at a neighbourhood gathering, but here they were, alone in the quiet serenity of the park.

"What are you doing here, Lucas?" Alex asked, his tone cautious yet open.

Lucas took a deep breath, steeling himself for what he was

about to say. "I needed to talk to you," he confessed, his voice barely above a whisper. "I need to apologize."

Alex turned to face Lucas, his expression a mix of surprise and wariness. He could see the turmoil etched on Lucas's face, a stark contrast to the bravado he usually displayed.

"What is it, Lucas?" Alex asked, his tone cautious yet open.

Lucas took a deep breath, steeling himself for what he was about to say. "I... I know I messed up, Alex. I never meant for any of this to happen. I never wanted Paul to get hurt."

Alex studied Lucas, his eyes searching for sincerity amidst the turmoil. He could see the genuine remorse in Lucas's eyes, a stark contrast to the tough exterior he usually wore.

"Lucas," Alex began, his voice soft but firm, "what happened... it wasn't just your fault. We were all involved in some way. But I appreciate you coming to me and owning up to your mistakes."

Lucas was taken aback as he had expected anger or blame, but instead, he found understanding and forgiveness.

"I'm so sorry, Alex," Lucas choked out, his voice thick with emotion. "I know I can't change the past, but I want to make things right. I want to do better."

Alex reached out, placing a comforting hand on Lucas's shoulder. "We all make mistakes, Lucas," he said gently. "What matters now is how we move forward from here. Let's focus on making things right."

Later that evening, as Alex sat at home with his mother, Joanna

Knight, he couldn't shake the memory of his conversation with Lucas. Though the wounds were still fresh, he found a glimmer of hope in the possibility of healing and reconciliation. As they reminisced about Paul's kindness and the memories they shared, Alex knew that love and forgiveness would guide them through even the darkest of times.

As the years passed and they grew into adulthood, Alex, Lucas, Marcus, and Scarlette found themselves navigating the complexities of life. Despite the passage of time and the distance that often separated them, they remained connected through the bonds forged in their shared history.

One evening, as they sat in their respective homes after a long day of work, their phones buzzed with excitement. With eager anticipation, they opened their messages, greeted by a flood of notifications from each other.

"Hey guys, it's been too long!" Alex's message read, his excitement palpable even through the screen.

"Absolutely! We should catch up soon," Lucas replied, his enthusiasm mirroring Alex's.

As they exchanged messages, reminiscing about old times and sharing updates on their lives, a sudden interruption shattered the tranquillity of their conversation. The news alerts on their phones blared with urgency, capturing their attention with headlines of chaos and destruction.

"Guys, have you seen this?" Scarlette's message flashed on their screens, accompanied by a link to a news article.

With growing apprehension, they clicked on the link, their

hearts sinking as they read the shocking reports. Mythical creatures, long thought to exist only in legends and folklore, were suddenly attacking London, wreaking havoc on the city streets.

As they watched the live news coverage, their minds raced with disbelief and fear. The once familiar landmarks of their beloved city were now engulfed in chaos, as people fled in terror from the monstrous creatures that roamed the streets.

"We have to do something," Marcus declared, his voice filled with determination. "London needs us."

With a shared sense of purpose, Alex, Lucas, Marcus, and Scarlette sprang into action, rallying together despite the miles that separated them. Though the challenges ahead were daunting, they knew that their bond, forged in the crucible of friendship and shared experiences, would give them the strength to face whatever trials lay ahead.

As they prepared to confront the mythical creatures that threatened their home, they drew strength from the knowledge that they were not alone. Together, they would stand against the darkness, united by the ties that bound them and the hope of a brighter tomorrow.

As the creatures invaded London, a tense encounter ensued between our heroes and one of the winged beasts. Here's a dialogue between them:

The creature swooped down from the darkened sky, its leathery wings beating with a menacing rhythm as it landed before Alex, Lucas, Marcus, and Scarlette, its eyes gleaming with a malevolent intelligence.

Alex tensed, gripping his weapon tightly as he faced the creature. "What are you?" he demanded, his voice steady despite the fear churning in his gut.

The creature let out a guttural hiss, its voice a low, rumbling growl that sent shivers down their spines. "We are the harbingers of chaos," it snarled, its breath reeking of sulfur and decay. "We are the bringers of destruction."

Lucas stepped forward, his jaw set with determination. "Why are you doing this?" he demanded, his voice echoing with defiance.

The creature's eyes narrowed, its gaze fixing on Lucas with an intensity that made his blood run cold. "We do as we please," it replied, its voice dripping with malice. "Your world is ours for the taking."

Marcus stepped up beside Lucas, his weapon at the ready. "Not if we have anything to say about it," he declared, his voice ringing with resolve.

The creature let out a guttural laugh, a sound that chilled them to the bone. "Foolish mortals," it sneered, its wings unfurling as it prepared to strike. "You cannot hope to stand against the might of the darkness."

Scarlette took a step forward, her eyes blazing with defiance. "We may be mortal," she said, her voice ringing with conviction, "but we will fight to protect our home and our loved ones, no matter the cost."

With a roar that shook the ground beneath their feet, the creature lunged forward, its talons poised to strike. But before it could reach them, Alex and his companions sprang into action, their weapons flashing in the darkness as they met the creature head-on in a clash of steel and shadow.

As the battle raged on, their determination never wavered, their voices raised in defiance against the encroaching darkness. And though the odds were stacked against them, they fought with a courage born of desperation, knowing that the fate of London, and perhaps the world itself, hung in the balance.

A few days later, Alex stood in his dimly lit room, the weight of the situation settled heavily upon him. Ruok's return was not just a resurgence of an old nemesis; it was a threat to everything he held dear. Memories of their past encounters flooded his mind, each one more perilous than the last. He couldn't afford to underestimate Ruok's intentions this time.

With a deep breath, Alex approached his cupboard, its wooden frame weathered by time. He hesitated for a moment before swinging it open, revealing the contents within. Among the clutter of forgotten items, his eyes fell upon the D-Blaster, its once gleaming surface now obscured by a layer of dust and neglect.

As he reached for the weapon, his fingers brushed against its cold metal, sending a shiver down his spine. This wasn't just any ordinary object; it was a symbol of the battles he thought he had left behind. But now, faced with the reality of Ruok's return, he knew he had no choice but to confront the danger head-on.

Turning to his wife, Alex struggled to find the right words to convey the gravity of the situation without causing her unnecessary worry. "Honey," he began, his voice betraying the turmoil raging within him, "I need to go out for a bit. There's... something I need to take care of."

His wife's brow furrowed with concern as she studied him, sensing the weight of his words. "Alex, what's going on?" she asked, her voice tinged with apprehension.

Alex hesitated, his gaze dropping to the floor as he grappled with how much to reveal. "It's... complicated," he replied finally, his tone heavy with resignation. "But I promise, I'll be back before you know it."

Her expression softened with understanding, though the worry in her eyes remained. "Please, Alex," she pleaded, reaching out to touch his arm, "be careful. I don't know what's going on, but I can sense that it's serious."

He nodded, grateful for her unwavering support even in the face of uncertainty. "I will," he assured her, giving her hand a reassuring squeeze. "I promise to do whatever it takes to keep us safe."

But as he turned to leave, Alex felt a pang of guilt gnaw at him. He couldn't bear the thought of leaving his wife alone, unaware of the danger that lurked in the shadows. Taking a deep breath, he turned back to face her, his resolve hardening.

"Listen," he said, his voice steady despite the turmoil churning inside him, "I need you to stay here. Lock the doors, close the curtains—don't let anyone in until I get back, understand?"

His wife's eyes widened with concern, her hand tightening around his. "Alex, what's going on? You're scaring me."

He forced a reassuring smile, though it felt hollow on his lips. "I can't explain right now, but trust me," he said, his voice firm, "I'll explain everything when I return. Just promise me you'll stay safe."

She nodded, her lips trembling with unspoken fear. "I promise," she whispered, her eyes never leaving his. "Please, Alex, just come back to me."

With a heavy heart, Alex pressed a kiss to her forehead before turning to leave once more. As he stepped out into the night, the weight of the D-Blaster hanging heavy at his side, he couldn't shake the sinking feeling that this time, things would be different. But one thing was certain: he would face whatever challenges lay ahead with courage and determination, for the sake of those he loved.

As Alex stepped into the cool night air, his mind raced with thoughts of the impending danger. The streets were quiet, bathed in the soft glow of streetlights casting long shadows across the pavement. He tightened his grip on the D-Blaster, the weight of it a constant reminder of the task that lay ahead.

With each step, the gravity of the situation pressed down on him like a heavy burden. Ruok's return meant that no one was safe, and Alex knew that he was the only one who could stop him. But the thought of facing his old nemesis filled him with a sense of dread, unlike anything he had ever experienced.

As he made his way through the deserted streets, his mind wandered back to the first time he had encountered Ruok. It had been years ago, a chance meeting that had quickly escalated into a battle for survival. Since then, they had crossed paths countless times, each confrontation more dangerous than the last.

But this time felt different. There was a sense of urgency in the air, a palpable tension that hung like a dark cloud over the city. Alex couldn't shake the feeling that Ruok was planning something big, something that could threaten the lives of everyone he held dear.

As he turned a corner, Alex spotted a group of figures huddled in the shadows, their faces obscured by the darkness. His heart pounded in his chest as he approached cautiously, the D-Blaster held at the ready. But as he drew closer, he realized that it was just a group of homeless people seeking shelter for the night.

Relief flooded through him as he lowered the weapon, the tension draining from his body like water from a leaky faucet. But even as he continued on his way, he couldn't shake the feeling of unease that gnawed at him from within.

Hours passed as Alex patrolled the streets, his senses alert for any sign of danger. But despite his vigilance, there was no sign of Ruok or his henchmen. It was as if they had vanished into thin air, leaving behind nothing but a trail of fear and uncertainty in their wake.

As dawn broke, Alex finally returned home, exhaustion weighing heavy on his weary limbs. His wife was waiting for him, her eyes filled with concern as she took in his haggard appearance.

"Alex, what happened?" she asked, her voice filled with worry.

He sighed heavily, the weight of the night pressing down on him like a leaden cloak. "I'm not sure," he admitted, his voice barely above a whisper. "But whatever it is, I fear that it's only just beginning."

As Alex sank into the nearest chair, his wife moved closer, her touch a soothing balm against the turmoil raging inside him. "You look exhausted," she murmured, her voice soft with concern. "What happened out there?"

He ran a hand through his hair, the events of the night replaying in his mind like a broken record. "It's Ruok," he confessed, his voice heavy with weariness. "He's back, and he's more dangerous than ever."

His wife's eyes widened in alarm, her hand tightening around his. "But I thought you dealt with him years ago," she said, her voice tinged with disbelief.

Alex nodded, the memories of their past encounters flashing before his eyes like scenes from a nightmare. "We thought we had," he admitted, his tone rueful. "But it seems he's returned with a vengeance, and this time, he won't stop until he gets what he wants."

His wife's brow furrowed with concern as she studied him, her gaze searching his face for any sign of reassurance. "What are you going to do?" she asked, her voice barely above a whisper.

Alex sighed heavily, the weight of the decision bearing down on him like a heavy burden. "I have to stop him," he said, his voice firm with determination. "I can't let him endanger our family or anyone else in this city."

His wife reached out to touch his face, her touch a gentle reminder of the love and support that surrounded him. "I understand," she said, her voice filled with unwavering faith. "Just promise me you'll be careful. I don't know what's going on, but I trust you to do whatever it takes to keep us safe."

Alex nodded, gratitude flooding through him at her steadfast belief in him. "I promise," he vowed, pressing a kiss to her forehead. "I won't let anything happen to you or our family. I'll do whatever it takes to stop Ruok and put an end to this madness once and for all."

With one last glance at his wife, Alex rose from his chair, the weight of responsibility settling heavy on his shoulders. As he stepped out into the morning light, the echoes of their conversation lingered in his mind like a silent prayer. But one thing was certain: he would face whatever challenges lay ahead with courage and determination, for the sake of those he loved.

Discover more about the author's inspirations, upcoming releases, and exclusive content at *www.andrormthompson.com*

Stay tuned for updates and explore the world behind the stories you love.

Printed in Great Britain
by Amazon

d3c5682e-2643-4539-adce-dbfba6a8f626R01